HEART SMASHER

REBELS OF RUSHMORE BOOK FOUR

MICHELLE HERCULES

INFINITE SKY PUBLISHING

Paperback ISBN: 978-1-959167-02-0

1

___

VANESSA – *Littleton, CA, 9 years ago*

A NUDGE on my arm startles me awake. I sit straighter and try to focus on what Father Medina is saying. *Try* being the key word here. Maybe I shouldn't have had a big lunch, but it's hard to resist my grandmother's *feijoada*. Beans, rice, and meat will put anyone to sleep. Pair that up with an unusually hot afternoon for California in March, and I'd need caffeine injected straight into my veins in order to stay awake. My friends from school think I'm crazy for drinking coffee, and their parents think *my* folks are crazy for letting Heather and me drink it. It's a cultural thing.

Why is the church so stuffy today? Its stucco walls are supposed to keep the heat out. Unlike most Catholic churches, this one isn't rich in decorations and frills—probably because the building is new.

I wipe my clammy forehead with the back of my hand and mutter, "Why is it so hot in here? Is Father Medina trying to turn us into stew?"

"Maybe only you. You shouldn't have eaten like a pig earlier," Heather retorts.

Jerk.

Someone snickers behind me, and I look over my shoulder to glower. It's Paris Andino, which means I can't really hold on to my annoyance for more than a second. I've known him for like forever. We always hang out at the Morales Country Club, and there's church. The boy is my kryptonite. How could he not be, with his tanned skin, dark hair, and the bluest pair of eyes I've ever seen, framed by ridiculously long lashes?

I don't realize I'm staring at him like an idiot until Heather elbows me again, giving me a new direction for my glare. "*What?*" I whisper-shout.

"Can you at least pretend to pay attention to the sermon?"

"It's not my fault Father Medina's voice is so monotonous." A yawn sneaks up on me.

"It *is* your fault for staying up late watching old soccer games," she retorts.

"I'm not going to apologize for having an interest in a worthwhile activity. Unlike you."

"You mean an obsession, right? Besides, I do plenty of worthwhile stuff."

"Preening in front of the mirror doesn't count, sis." I smirk.

Paris chuckles again, and this time, Heather is the one who looks over her shoulder. "Can it, Andino."

Father Medina clears his throat, scowling. At least, for once, his annoyance isn't directed at me. Heather faces forward again and slouches. As the twin who never gets in trouble, she hates being scolded. Her face is now redder than a tomato.

The sermon continues for another fifteen minutes without any more interruptions, which is a miracle considering the audience is all teenagers who, like me, were probably strong-armed into going through confirmation. I manage to stay awake, thanks to the knowledge that Paris is right behind me. My tummy is filled with crazy butterflies.

We're supposed to break into groups now and discuss the lesson given during the sermon, but I have to pee badly, so first I head to the secondary building where the restrooms are. Mercifully, Heather doesn't come with me. No doubt she would take the opportunity to lay all the blame for what happened earlier on me.

I'm distracted when I walk out of the restroom, so when Paris's voice echoes in the hallway, I jump back, startled.

I press a hand to my chest. "Jeez, you almost gave me a heart attack."

"Sorry. I didn't mean to scare you." He smiles, revealing his adorable dimples.

A blush creeps onto my cheeks while my heart speeds up like a midfielder who just snagged the ball from the opposing team and has a clear path to the goal.

Keep it cool, Vanessa. Keep it cool.

"Are you waiting for someone?"

"Yeah. You."

My idiotic heart skips a beat. I croak, "Me? Why?"

"On a scale of one to ten, how mad is Heather right now?"

Disappointment floods through me. Did Paris just corner me to ask about my sister? I'm used to Heather getting all the attention from boys at school. She's blonde, beautiful, and has already developed all her assets, unlike me. I seem destined to have an athletic frame, which usually works for me. Right now, however, jealousy is coursing through me.

I cross my arms and frown. "Why do you care?"

Paris's smile wilts a fraction. "I don't care. I mean, I thought maybe you needed a break from her, if she's acting like a total dragon."

My irritation dissipates like magic. I was already getting a break from her, but he doesn't know that.

"What do you have in mind?" I ask.

His lips curl into a mischievous grin. "I can't tell you. It's top secret."

"So... what? Am I supposed to just follow you blindly?"

"Yeah. I promise it'll be cool."

Little does he know I'd follow him even if he was planning to open the gates of Hell.

God. That was dramatic. I think Heather's antics are rubbing off on me.

Waving my hand in a carefree way, I reply, "Fine. Lead the way."

His grin widens into a broad smile that makes my heart skip a beat. He doesn't say anything else, just veers in the opposite direction of where the group meetings are taking place. He has long legs, so I follow a bit behind him, which allows me to check him out. Unlike other thirteen-year-olds, Paris isn't scrawny. That's probably because of football. I've heard he's already the most popular boy at All Saints, the private middle school he goes to. We're in the same grade, but Heather and I attend public school.

I'm lost in admiring his tush and don't notice that he's led me out of the secondary building and to the back of the church. Cory, his older brother, is standing near a sycamore tree, looking hella suspicious.

"Did you get it?" Paris asks.

"Mathias hasn't come out yet."

"Uh, get what?" I butt in.

No sooner do I ask than Cory's friend walks out the back door, holding a bottle of red wine. *Crap.*

"You're joking, right?" I blurt out.

"Aw, come on, Vanessa. Don't tell me you're Miss Goody Two-shoes like your sister," Mathias pipes up.

"Please. I'm nothing like Heather." I turn to Paris. "You said this was gonna be cool."

His face falls, and I regret my words.

"You don't need to drink any," Mathias says before pulling the cork free with his teeth.

I've never tasted wine before, and I *am* a little curious. But the idea also makes me leery. The image of Aunt Marietta drunk at every family gathering has made me less keen to try alcohol.

Mathias takes a big chug of the wine and then passes the bottle to Cory, who follows his friend's example. I'm surprised to see him breaking the rules. I always pegged him as the responsible older brother. He drinks way more than Mathias, as if he wants to get wasted at any cost. When he finally lowers the bottle, I wonder if there's anything left. He wipes his mouth with the back of his hand but doesn't make a motion to return the bottle to his friend.

"Did you leave any for us?" Paris takes the bottle from Cory.

"Yeah, yeah, little bro. Still plenty for you and your girlfriend."

I gasp, and Paris replies quickly, "She's not my girlfriend."

My face is burning up, and I'm glad I don't blush as obviously as Heather does.

"Yeah, that'd be gross," I say.

Cory and Mathias laugh. I don't dare glance at Paris to see his reaction, so I look at my shoes instead. After a moment, Paris nudges my arm, forcing me to turn to him.

"Want some?" He offers me the bottle.

I wasn't planning to drink, but to recover from embarrassment, I accept the offer and bring the bottle's rim to my lips. The first sip almost makes me gag. I force it down, not wanting to increase my humiliation. The second gulp is larger and, as the alcohol goes down my throat, I begin to relax. I can't possibly be getting drunk already, can I?

"Hey! What are you kids doing back there?" someone yells in the distance.

I pivot on the spot, hiding the bottle of wine behind my back.

"Shit! That's one of the coordinators," Mathias blurts out. "Scram."

He and Cory take off toward the midsize public park next to the church grounds. I'm frozen, not knowing what to do. If the coordinator catches me with the wine, I'm screwed. My parents will flay me alive.

Paris takes my hand and tugs it. "Come on. We have to get out of here."

I let him steer me in the direction of the park. We run side by side, and I'm glad that, thanks to soccer, I can keep up with him and his extremely long legs. We've lost Cory and Mathias already, but we don't stop running until we reach the old tree house, deep in the forest. We don't go up, as it might fall apart at any moment. No one comes here save for teenagers looking for trouble.

Oh, that's us.

"Jesus! That was close." Paris drops my hand and then rests both of his on his knees as he catches his breath.

I'm not as winded as he is, and that fills my chest with pride. "At least we got the wine," I say.

He grins. "Hand it over. I'm parched."

I pass the bottle to him, but not before I take another sip. It doesn't taste as bad now. For a few minutes, we keep taking turns until the bottle is empty.

"I'm still thirsty," I say.

"Yeah, I don't think alcohol really helps with that."

"How long do you think we should stay hidden?" I glance at the sky, noticing it's already turning orange.

"We have to get back before our parents come to pick us up."

I shove my hands in my pockets. "Do you think the coordinator recognized us?"

His face twists into a grimace. "It's possible."

"Crap." I look away, thinking about what my punishment will be for ditching Bible study and getting drunk. My stomach feels queasy with the possibility that my parents might take soccer away from me.

Paris touches my shoulder. "Don't worry. If you get in trouble, I'll take full responsibility."

"That's not fair. No one forced me to skip class and drink wine."

He steps closer to me, making my breath hitch. "True, but I had ulterior motives for inviting you to tag along."

"What ulterior motives?" I whisper.

"Uh, getting you alone."

My brows shoot to the heavens. "You're not planning to kill me, are you?"

"What? No." He rubs the back of his neck. "I'm making a mess of things, and I don't think it has anything to do with the wine."

"You're not making any sense."

"I like you, Vanessa."

My jaw drops. Paris Andino *likes* me? Am I dreaming? Or maybe I'm having a drunken vision.

He steps toward me, his expression already falling. "I'm sorry. It was stupid of m—"

I jump into his space and throw my arms around his neck... and then I kiss him on the lips. He tenses, but then his arms wrap around my waist. That's as far as my drunken impulsiveness goes, though. I've never kissed anyone in my life, and I have no idea what to do next. I begin to pull back, but Paris frames my face with his hands and then teases my lips open with his tongue. Holy *shit*. I'm French kissing Paris Andino. Someone pinch me. I have no idea what I'm doing, but thanks to the wine, I'm not freaking out too much about it.

"Vanessa Cristine Castro!" My mother's shrill voice cuts through the air.

Paris and I jump apart and turn. My parents are standing not too far from us, and with them, Paris's parents and Cory. *Oh my god.* I want a hole to open and swallow me. Mom's shrewd gaze zeroes in on the discarded wine bottle at our feet, and then it's freaking Armageddon.

That's it. I'll be grounded for life.

2

PARIS

"I can't believe you two!" my father yells from behind his desk. "I can't tell you how disappointed I am in your behavior."

I wince in my chair, trying to appear smaller, something that's almost impossible when I'm already almost five foot nine. Our father is mostly a calm person, but when he loses his temper, he *loses his temper*. Sadly, that's been happening more frequently, and Cory is often the target of his wrath.

"It was my idea, Dad. Just punish me," my brother says.

I shake my head, not willing to let him take the fall alone. "I drank the wine too."

Dad slams his open palm on the mahogany desk, shaking the two picture frames on it. "Enough! Both of you are grounded for a month. It's school and home."

"What about football?" I ask.

"You're the star of the team, I'm not going to screw over Coach Smith because you acted like an idiot. You can still play, but that's it. No going out for pizza with your teammates after a game."

That's going to suck, but at least I can still play.

I slouch in my chair, and reply meekly, "Okay."

"Will that also apply to my extracurricular activities?" Cory asks.

There's an edge to his tone, which means I might witness another argument between him and Dad. They've been at odds since he told us he wasn't playing football in high school. He wanted to pursue other interests. I believe Dad would have been okay with that—he isn't a crazy sports fan—if Cory's new interest wasn't art. He wants to pursue painting, and according to my parents, that's not a career.

"No. Your canvases and paint brushes will survive not being used for a month."

"I have a field trip to New York in two weeks. It's paid for."

Dad leans back in his plush leather chair. "You should have thought about that before you decided to steal Father Medina's wine."

"That's bullshit!" Cory jumps to his feet, almost sending his own chair tumbling back.

Dad's spine goes taut as he points a finger at Cory. "You just earned another week of punishment."

"Whatever." He stalks out of the office and bangs the door shut.

I'm not sure what to do. Cory used to be the role model for the perfect son. He never raised his voice and always did what he was told. But ever since he started high school, it's like he turned into a different person. Or a switch was flipped.

Dad pinches the bridge of his nose. "What's going on with your brother, Paris?"

"I don't know."

He picks up a framed photo of Cory and me. "I hardly recognize my own son."

"Maybe you could let him go to New York, I mean, since you're letting me play—"

"No, absolutely not." He sets the picture frame down. "He's out of control. What I need to do is tighten the leash."

"I think he's just angry that you're not being supportive of his new interests. I mean, artists can make a lot of money, and he might change his mind later."

"That's the problem, son. Your brother went from being an *A* student to someone who doesn't care about anything besides getting into trouble. You'd tell me if your brother was taking drugs, wouldn't you?"

I swallow the lump in my throat. I refuse to believe Cory would be involved with drugs. "I don't think he is, Dad. Truly."

"It's a good thing you're still at All Saints. I knew we should have kept Cory in private school."

I have no comment to that. The only private school in Littleton that goes through high school is as expensive as an Ivy League college. My parents have money, but not that kind of money.

"How long do you think Mom will stay mad at the Castros?" I ask to change the subject, and also because I want to know if it'd be safe to ask Vanessa to be my girlfriend.

She doesn't go to All Saints, and the only chance I get to see her is at church. But if my parents aren't on speaking terms with hers, getting her alone again will be hard. I was kicked out of the youth program—not that I cared about confirmation anyway.

Dad gives me a droll look. "Have you met your mother? The Castros will stay on her blacklist until she dies."

Great.

"May I be excused?" I ask.

He waves his hand. "Yes. And Paris, please don't go looking for more trouble, okay? I can't deal with two rebel sons."

"I won't," I lie.

There's no chance I'm going to give up on Vanessa. But before I contact her, I should probably wait until the dust settles. She doesn't have a cell phone, and she isn't on social media. I have no choice but to wait for another opportunity to get her alone.

3

VANESSA – *Two weeks later*

I HAVEN'T SEEN or heard from Paris in two weeks. He and Cory didn't attend service the Sunday following the wine incident, so I had to bear all the judgmental glances alone. I'm glad that the gossip in my school lasted only a couple of days, and it wasn't bad. Mostly the girls wanted to know what kissing Paris Andino was like. Yeah, he's popular in my school too.

Maybe the kiss didn't mean anything to him, or I sucked at it. Schoolwork and soccer practice keep me busy though, and the days begin to blend together. I can't say that I don't think about him, and on occasion, my mother will bring up Paris's mother during dinner by calling her that "horrible woman," and one of those instances is now.

"I saw her at the supermarket today. She has an assistant to help her with groceries. An assistant!" She gestures wildly with her hands.

"Maybe she was buying a lot of things, honey," Dad replies calmly.

It's an English-only day in our house, which means Mom's tirade won't be as colorful as it would if she were speaking Portuguese. My parents moved from Rio de Janeiro to California just after they got married, because Dad received an amazing job offer. Heather and I were born in California, and we went through a phase growing up when we refused to speak Portuguese even though we had other family members living nearby. I guess a lot of bilingual kids go through that. But now that we speak both languages fluently, my parents decided it would be good for Mom to practice her English more, since she's less exposed to it—most of her friends speak either Portuguese or Spanish.

"She has two sons. Why can't they help her? It's in poor taste, I tell you."

"I heard they're still grounded," Heather pipes up.

I whip around to her. "Who told you that?"

"Tara Carmichael. Her parents are friends with one of the Andinos' neighbors. The Andinos were at the party but without Paris and Cory."

"Maybe they didn't want to go to the party."

"Well, the hosts' daughter, some girl named Lydia, goes to All Saints as well, and she confirmed that Paris is only allowed to leave the house for school and football."

Mom snorts. "That's the least punishment that pervert should get for trying to corrupt Vanessa."

My face heats in a flash. I drop my gaze to my plate and cease asking questions about Paris. But Heather seems determined to keep talking about him.

While Mom continues to talk about her day, Heather leans close and whispers in my ear. "You have competition, sis. Tara told me this Lydia chick all but implied she's Paris's girlfriend."

I clutch the fork and knife tighter. "Whatever. I don't care."

"Right. Well, it's good if you don't. He's cute and all, but he isn't the last cookie in the package."

The food tastes like ashes now, and I can barely swallow.

Not much later, the doorbell rings several times in a row, and when we don't get to the door yet, the knocking comes.

"Oh my god. What now?" Mom gets up in a huff and strides toward the front of the house.

Since I've lost my appetite, I follow her to see what the commotion's about.

Aunt Marietta storms in like a freaking hurricane, carrying several shopping bags. She's my mother's cousin, but Heather and I call her aunt. I'm not sure why she brought all the bags into the house instead of leaving them in her car, until I realize she probably came by taxi so she could drink during her shopping spree.

"What are you doing here, Marietta?" Mom asks.

"*Prima, babado fortíssimo pra te contar,*" she starts in Portuguese.

Mom doesn't really care for her, and with a scowl firmly in place, she replies, "In English, please."

"Fine! Well, I was doing some shopping downtown when I heard the most awful news. One of the Andino boys is dead."

My blood freezes in my veins, and it feels like I'm falling into the hole that opened underneath my feet.

"Oh my god. Which one?" Mom asks, pressing a hand against her chest. Like she cares.

"I think the oldest. Dreadful thing. Apparently he killed himself and the younger one found the body." She makes the sign of the cross as if she were a religious person. I feel like yelling at her, demanding more information, but I can't find my voice.

Heather pulls me into a side hug. I didn't notice her walking over.

"That's terrible news," Dad says.

"I need to see Paris," I blurt out.

Everyone looks at me as if I just sprouted a second head.

"You're not leaving this house, young lady," Mom retorts.

"Mom, please. Now is not the time for pettiness," I beg.

She widens her eyes. "I'm not being petty. It's not appropriate, Vanessa."

"Your mother is right, honey. We don't know when this happened, and I'm pretty sure everyone is still in shock. You should wait until tomorrow."

My vision is blurry with unshed tears. I turn around and run upstairs before they can see me cry my eyes out. I dive onto my bed and hide my face under a pillow. My heart is breaking for Paris and his family. I didn't spend as much time with Cory as I did with Paris, but he was always nice to me. Why would he kill himself? He was always in a good mood, always had a smile on his face.

Heather comes in and sits on the edge of my mattress. "It's going to be okay, Nessa."

She never calls me by that nickname unless I'm hurt, like when I get injured playing soccer. I'd trade physical pain for this agony burning in my chest any time.

"He lost his brother, Heather. How can that be okay?"

"It won't be for a long time, but eventually, it will get better."

I turn around, wiping the moisture from my cheeks. "I need to see Paris tonight."

"Are you sure? Maybe you should wait until tomorrow, like Dad said."

Determined now, I sit up. "No. I'm going tonight. Will you cover for me?"

"How do you plan to get there?"

"By bike. It's not that far."

"Do you remember the way?"

I went to Paris's house once last year, before our folks became mortal enemies.

I nod. "I think so."

She studies me for a couple seconds before she replies, "Okay."

I don't waste a minute. I put on a hoodie and then a pair of sneakers before Heather and I tiptoe down the stairs. Aunt Marietta is still talking nonstop. Everyone is in the living room, leaving the path to the garage door clear. It's torture, walking slowly to avoid making noise, but eventually I get to the garage.

"I'll tell everyone you're not feeling well," Heather says before I take off.

"Thank you. I owe you one."

"Yes, you do. I hope you get to see Paris. If you do, tell him I'm sorry too."

Her words make me choke, and almost reignite the tears. But I can't cry, not now when I need clear vision.

I pedal as fast as I can, hoping not to get lost. I remember a few landmarks that help guide me, but it's already dark, and I'm afraid I might miss a turn. I sharpen my focus, and just when I think I've gone too far, I see a familiar car signal to turn right. It's Father Medina's car. He must be going to Paris's house.

It turns out he was heading to the same destination, because when I get there, he's already parked and left the car. But I recognize the neighborhood and the house's brick exterior and red door.

My heart is about to leap out of my throat and my breaths come in bursts. I remove my helmet and stride toward Paris's front door. I'm shaking, suddenly afraid that my presence will only make things worse.

I finally gather the courage to ring the doorbell, and then I wait on pins and needles. I expect Paris's mother to answer the door, or perhaps her assistant, but instead it's a girl my age.

"Whatever you're selling, now is not a good time," she says with an air of arrogance.

Who the hell is she?

"I'm not selling anything. I'm Paris's friend. I came to see him."

Her eyes narrow as if what I said offended her. "Well, he can't see anyone right now."

"You don't know that," I retort, not willing to be sent away by this annoying stranger.

"Lydia, who is it?" a female voice asks from inside the house.

Hell, this is the neighbor who claims she's Paris's girlfriend. Maybe she is. Why else would she be here?

She looks over her shoulder, and replies, "Some girl who wants to see Paris. I told her he can't see anyone right now."

A woman in her fifties bearing a strong resemblance to Paris's mother joins the obnoxious girl blocking my way. Her eyes are red and puffy. "I'm sorry, dear, but he's not in any shape to see anyone at the moment. I'll tell him you stopped by, okay? What's your name?"

"It's Vanessa Castro. When do you think I can talk to him?"

Her face crumples, and I think she's on the verge of crying. "It's hard to say. Why don't you call the house first before dropping by?"

"Okay. I'll do that."

She shuts the door in my face before I have a chance to step back. Now I'm heartbroken and jealous as hell. With heavy feet and an even heavier heart, I trudge back to my bike. A sense of numbness washes over me. I ignore the thunder and lightning that sparks in the sky, and the rain that drenches me in a matter of seconds. I take a sharp curve going too fast and lose control.

The last things I remember are approaching headlights and the sound of tires screeching.

4

VANESSA - *PRESENT DAY*

THE JOHN RUSHMORE main cafeteria is as busy as ever, despite the time of the day. There are smaller dining halls in different buildings, but this is the one most of the student body prefers, mainly because the jocks and Greeks prefer it and are here at all hours. I come here because the food is better. It's way past lunchtime and I don't know what all these people are still doing here. Today, I'm not in the mood to brave the crowds, though. Honestly, I'd have gone to a fast-food joint, but Coach Lauda has put all of us on a healthy diet, so I have to set the example for the girls. After all, I'm team captain.

Joanne is the last to join us at the table, and her tray has enough food for at least three football players.

"What's all that?" Steff, our keeper, asks.

"I'm trying to eat things I've never had before," she grumbles.

"And you decided to eat them all at once?" I ask through a chuckle.

"I'm pretty sure I'll hate eighty percent of what I got, and I really don't want to stand in that huge line again. Why is it still so busy?"

"Who knows? Maybe the football gods are making an appearance," Steff replies without hiding her sarcasm.

I don't have anything against the Rebels, save for one particular player. Paris Andino and I have a history—something no one on my team knows, and I plan to keep it that way. I'd die of embarrassment if they found out he was my first kiss and that, later, he pretended I didn't exist.

Jackass.

I inspect Joanne's tray carefully, noticing her selection is not that eclectic. I see an egg salad sandwich, a falafel, a pyro with Greek salad, and a regular ham and cheese sub.

"Why do you think you need to change how you eat?" Phoebe asks, tossing her multicolored hair over her shoulder.

"I've been told I'm a picky eater."

I trade a glance with Steff. Could the person who said that be Joanne's mysterious girlfriend?

"Where's Sadie?" Charlotte chimes in. "I thought she was joining us."

"Didn't you see her message in the group chat?" Joanne asks.

When Charlotte gives her a blank stare, I add, "She was running late, which is code for she got busy with Danny."

"Those crazy kids have been going at each other like two horny rabbits. It's a miracle they have any energy left for sports," Steff pipes up, right before she shoves a piece of chocolate in her mouth.

"Hey, what's that?" I glower.

Her eyes widen innocently, but the corners of her mouth twitch up. "What?"

"I saw that piece of chocolate, Steff. We're all supposed to be eating healthier during the week," I retort, more angrily than is warranted.

I want a piece of chocolate, damn it. I'm about the get my period, and the craving is bad. I'm pretty sure I'll cave at home, because now that I saw her eat some, my mouth is watering. I stare at my fruit salad and feel depressed. I so don't want to eat that right now.

The chat continues, but I notice Phoebe is staring at her plate of food with a downcast expression. She seems paler too.

I reach across the table and touch her hand. "Hey, are you okay?"

She looks up. "Yeah. I think I need some orange juice to wash down my sandwich."

She gets up before I can offer to tag along. I keep my eyes trained on her though. She looked like she was about to pass out. Once she's out of the area with all the tables, she seems to trip over something and staggers forward, right into the arms of Paris.

Hell. I knew something was off. I jump out of my seat and make a beeline toward her. But an entire table decides to vacate just then, and several people end up blocking my way. It takes me a few extra seconds to reach them, and by the time I do, Lydia is there, yelling at poor Phoebe.

Son of a bitch.

"What's going on here?" I ask, not hiding my aggravation.

Phoebe puts her hand on her forehead and sways a little. Shit. She *is* sick. I step next to her and take her arm, steadying her.

"It's nothing," Paris replies.

"Nothing my ass," Lydia shrieks. "That girl was all over your space, Paris."

"I tripped," Phoebe replies feebly.

"Are you okay, hon?" I ask her, ignoring Lydia Bitch Face.

"I need to use the restroom."

"Okay. Let's go."

"Keep your players away from Paris, Vanessa," Lydia sneers.

I whip my face in her direction. "Fuck off, Lydia."

"Hey, that wasn't necessary." Paris comes to his girlfriend's defense, making my blood boil.

I switch my death glare to him. "Keep a leash on your bitchy girlfriend, Paris. You may be a pussy when it comes to her, but no one else is."

PARIS

I swallow the retort that bubbles up my throat as I watch Vanessa steer her teammate away from us. Her long dark hair is pulled back into a high ponytail, and it sways back and forth in a hypnotic way. I should look away, but I can't. She's always had that power over me. I don't know who I'm more angry at right now—Vanessa or myself. I should aim my annoyance at Lydia, but she's out of control like that because I let her get away with shit. Her antics are getting old and making it much harder to remember why I put up with them in the first place.

"I can't believe you let that bitch talk to us like that," Lydia complains.

"What did you want me to do? Curse at them, start a fight? You're the one who caused the drama." I turn around and head for the cafeteria's exit.

I sense several pairs of eyes staring at us. As usual, Lydia created a circus, and I'm once again the clown in her show.

"She had her hands all over you. I'm sick and tired of bimbos coming on to you."

I push the door open with excessive force and increase my pace. Lydia has to run to keep up with me.

"She tripped. I just happened to be in her way," I grit out.

"Whatever. I don't buy it."

I stop suddenly and whirl around. We're now in the middle of the quad, and there are fewer people around. "You need to stop with this nonsense, Lydia."

Her doe eyes widen and become brighter. Damn it. Here come the waterworks.

"I can't stop it. Every girl on campus wants to take you away from me. No one cares that you have a girlfriend. How do you think that makes me feel?"

"I can't help what other people do. I'm with you, and you need to trust me. I never give you any reason to be jealous."

The tears roll down her cheeks. Any other time, I'd pull her into a hug and console her. But I'm finally beginning to see her behavior as pure manipulation. Still, I hesitate. There's a part of me that fears her over-the-top reaction is out of her control. I remember that horrible day when I found Cory unresponsive. My stomach twists into painful knots.

Lydia wipes her tears with a jerky swipe of her fingers and then gives her back to me. Her entire body is shaking.

Hell.

I walk over and pull her back to my chest. "Please don't cry."

"I can't help it. I've been under so much stress. Do you know how hard it is to get into a good medical program?"

"Uh, I'm premed too, remember?" I turn her around in my arms and tuck a loose strand of hair behind her ear.

Her expression softens, and then she rises on her tiptoes and presses her lips to mine.

There was a time when her kisses would spread warmth through my chest. Now, my heart constricts painfully. I know it's over, but how do I tell her when she's already spiraling?

Cory's death might not have been my fault, but if I end things with Lydia now and she does something drastic, I'll never forgive myself.

5

VANESSA - *1 week later*

As I walk across the Morales Country Club parking lot, I tug down the hem of my dress. The fabric itches and I hate the color—a burnt orange that makes me look like a pumpkin—but I can't complain. If I had gone shopping with Mom and Heather in Littleton last month, I would have been able to choose something more my style. Our hometown isn't far from LA, where John Rushmore University is located, but when it comes to my family, the notion of a quick visit doesn't exist.

"Stop fidgeting, Vanessa. You look like you have fleas," Mom complains.

Heather snickers. "Maybe she does."

"Shut your face, Heather."

"Girls, can you please not bicker tonight?" Dad asks in his patient voice.

"What's this dress made of? Pine needles?" I turn to my mother.

She rolls her eyes. "It's gorgeous. Just stand straighter and think about how much fun you'll have tonight."

Unlikely. Coming to these stuffy parties at my parents' club is a pain in my ass. Not even Heather seems to enjoy them anymore—probably because she already dated all the cute guys from the club throughout high school. And most of them won't be back home for this anyway, since many went to out-of-state colleges. Heather and I both got scholarships to attend Rushmore—I got one for soccer, and Heather for cheerleading —so going there was a no-brainer. Besides, Rushmore is an excellent school. The only drawback is its closeness to Littleton.

Inside the main building, we follow the herd of new arrivals to the reception area, where high tables have been strategically distributed and waiters are serving canapés and glasses of champagne. Heather and I each take a glass, and while our folks are distracted greeting old friends, we go in different directions and blend in with the crowd. I find a corner where no one can disturb me and pull out my cell phone.

The Ravens group chat is quiet tonight, and I think that has to do with the gruesome training session we had today. My legs aren't *too* sore yet, but tomorrow is going to be murder.

ME: How is everyone tonight?

SADIE: I want to die.

JOANNE: Same. I can't feel my legs.

STEFF: You guys are a bunch of whiny babies. I'm fine.

I see that Sadie starts typing a reply but decides not to send the message in the end. A grin tugs the corners of my lips. I bet she was typing something sassy and thought better of it. I take a sip of my drink and type my response.

ME: Make sure you rest tonight, especially you, Sadie.

SADIE: Bloody hell. Why are you singling me out?

STEFF: Maybe because of your bedroom activities. 🍆

SADIE: Don't be haters because you aren't getting any. Besides, Danny is great with his tongue.

JOANNE: Whoa. TMI, sister.

A bubble of laughter goes up my throat. I knew chatting with the girls would lift my spirits.

"What's so funny?" a male voice asks.

I tense, knowing who I'm going to find standing in front of me. Paris fucking Andino.

"None of your business." I swipe away the group-chat screen and lower my phone.

"You're mad at me. Is it because of the cafeteria incident?" he asks, seeming unfazed by my harsh reply.

Ignoring his asinine question, I ask one of my own. "Where's your girlfriend? Am I going to be called a tramp because you're talking to me?"

Guilt seems to shine in his eyes. It was the same look he gave me when we got caught making out in the forest after drinking all that wine. "She's not here." His voice is tight and cold.

"Pity. I was looking forward to another lovely conversation with her."

"I didn't come here to argue with you. Yeah, what Lydia said was shitty, but—"

"There's no *but*, Paris. Your girlfriend is a heinous bitch, and I don't know what's more pathetic—the fact that you put up with it, or that you actually defend her actions."

He runs his fingers through his hair and sighs. "You don't know what's going on, okay? I'm trying my best to do the right thing."

His confession gives me pause. "Why? What kind of hold does Lydia have over you?"

He swallows hard, making his Adam's apple bob up and down. "For starters, she was there for me when I needed it most."

My stomach drops through the earth. He must be referring

to when he lost his brother. I touch the scar near my elbow, remembering that day.

"That's hardly a reason to stay with someone," I reply.

Paris's hard gaze stays on my face as he clenches his jaw. I want to know what he's thinking, but the moment is interrupted by his phone's ringtone. I can guess who's calling him.

He answers the call with a "Hey baby," and that's my cue to leave. I can't handle listening to his conversation. It's puke inducing.

I don't go far before Heather finds me.

"What did Paris want?" she asks.

"I have no clue."

"Riiight." She narrows her eyes. "Tell me, sis. Why do you dislike his girlfriend so much? Is it because she's a bitch, or because she's dating the guy you like?"

"Do you seriously think I care who Paris dates? He was just a stupid crush when I was thirteen."

She gives me a droll look. "Come on, you disobeyed our parents and rode off on your bike during a downpour to get to that boy. You even got a scar as a result. He was more than a crush, and you aren't over him yet."

Heather walks away before I can refute her theory. There's no point though. She isn't wrong. I don't think I'm over Paris, which is crazy. It's been *nine years*, for crying out loud. A first kiss shouldn't carry that much weight. I thought focusing on soccer would be enough to make me forget about him, but apparently not. To get over someone, you need to get under someone else. Which means...

I need a boyfriend.

PARIS

. . .

I SHOULD HAVE KNOWN Lydia wouldn't allow me to enjoy an evening without her. She couldn't attend the charity gala with me and my parents tonight because she has to study. I could have given them an excuse and not come, but I was hoping Vanessa would be here. Like me, she often gets roped into family events. I wasn't wrong, but as usual, our conversation went south fast.

I'm annoyed—or rather, conflicted as hell—about my motives for being at this party. Dealing with Lydia on top of everything is not what I want. She calls, citing a panic attack, and she's alone in her dorm room. I'm already feeling guilty. I went to talk to Vanessa with the excuse of apologizing, but the truth is, I just wanted to be near her. I'm not sure what it is about her, but every time we interact—meaning argue—it brings back feelings I thought I had buried a long time ago. She was my first crush, my first kiss, and truth be told, I've never gotten over her.

Hence why I walk out of the party without telling my folks I'm leaving. We didn't come together, which allows me to sneak out.

No sooner do I get behind the steering wheel of my truck than heavy rain begins to fall, creating a curtain of water around me. I drive carefully, especially since I've had a few drinks already.

Shit. This wasn't a smart move, Paris.

I decide to park and wait for the rain to lessen. As I look for a safe place to pull over, something darts in front of my truck, and in a knee-jerk reaction, I turn the wheel sharply to my right to avoid running over whatever it is. The tires lose traction, and the truck spins out of control. My pulse skyrockets as I attempt to stop what's happening, which is pointless. The truck crashes against something solid, and pain explodes all over my face thanks to the airbag.

My breath comes in bursts, and it takes a moment for my heart to stop trying to jump out of my chest. When the shock begins to dissipate, the sound of an approaching siren makes me tense. Hell. If the cops ask me to take a breathalyzer test, I'm screwed. I throw my head against the headrest, close my eyes, and think about how I put myself in this situation.

Vanessa's parting words come to the forefront of my mind. Being with Lydia because she helped me through tough times is not an excuse to stay with her. It's been a while since she cared about anything other than herself.

The siren stops, and a car door opens. Johnny Law is here. I open my eyes and, a moment later, he's standing just outside my window.

"Are you okay there, son?"

I lower the window and face my doom. "I've had better evenings."

"The ambulance is on its way." He narrows his eyes. "You're on the Rebels football team, aren't you? Paris Andino?"

I know there are quite a number of Rebels fans in Littleton, but I'm a bit surprised the cop is one of them.

"Yes, sir."

He rubs his face, looking worried. "Can you move your legs and arms?"

"I don't think I broke anything."

"Good. Good. Don't worry, son. We'll get you out of here in one piece."

He doesn't even ask if I've been drinking. I can't believe my luck. I close my eyes and send a little prayer to whatever is out there. It seems my ill-fated decision will not ruin my life after all. But it definitely brought much-needed clarity.

This accident might not end my career, but it'll definitely be the end of something else.

6

PARIS - *6 months later*

MY PHONE VIBRATES in my pocket. It's the only reason I notice it's ringing. The bar is too crowded and loud. Not surprising, considering Tailgaters has a two-for-one special tonight. I check my phone, and when I see who's calling, I shove it right back in. Lydia has been blowing it up ever since she returned from her retreat in Colorado, and after a peaceful summer of being single and drama-free, I'm not keen to let her back into my life. Our breakup was not an easy one. There were tears, and suicide threats. I had to get her parents involved, because I was done carrying the burden alone. I feel some remorse over it, but I have to put myself first. It's the first week of my senior year at Rushmore, and I want to enjoy it.

"Your pants are shaking, bro," Andreas pipes up.

I take a sip of my beer before replying. "I know. It's Lydia again."

"Oh shit. She's back from Colorado, right?" Danny asks.

"Yep."

"I don't blame you for avoiding her. I know too well what it's like to be in a toxic relationship." Danny shudders.

My teammates never hid that they didn't like my ex very much. Andreas was the most vocal about his dislike. Danny tried to be more diplomatic. But since I broke up with Lydia, everyone stopped walking on eggshells when the topic was her.

"Well, you have Sadie now," I say, genuinely happy for him.

"Yeah." His face splits into a goofy grin, making him look younger than he is. He just turned twenty-one, but I still see him as the baby of the team.

All my friends have awesome girlfriends, and I'm not the least bit jealous. Truth be told, I don't want to jump into another serious relationship until I'm thirty and my parents start to get on my nerves about settling down. I want to know what it's like to live without worrying about someone else.

Andreas throws his arm over Danny's shoulder. "We got the golden ticket, Danny Boy." He looks sheepishly at me. "Ah, sorry, dude. You're going to find your special girl too. Don't worry."

I open my mouth to say I'm in no hurry when I catch sight of Vanessa Castro across the room. She's with her loser boyfriend, and I'm not sure why, but seeing them together puts me in a foul mood.

"What are you staring at?" Andreas asks, following my line of vision. "Ah, maybe Paris has already found his target."

I glower. "Shut your mouth, Rossi."

His eyes widen. "Jesus, will you relax? I was just kidding. I know you two are like cats and dogs."

"But sometimes that's the attraction, isn't it? Enemies to lovers and all," Danny chimes in.

"Come again?" Andreas raises an eyebrow. "Are you reading Sadie's romance novels?"

Danny scoffs. "Sadie doesn't read romance, but so you

know, enemies to lovers is a universal trope found in other genres outside of romance."

"Sure, sure." Andreas laughs.

"Don't listen to him. Everyone knows Rossi is an uncultured swine."

"What the fuck, Andino," Andreas retorts.

I finish the rest of my beer and tell them I'm getting another round. Then I make my way to the bar. After I catch the bartender's attention, my gaze wanders to Vanessa and her boyfriend on the other side of it. She seems tense, and the douche looks unhappy about something. It looks like they're having an argument, but it's impossible to hear anything over the loud music blasting from the speakers.

I shouldn't stare. Couples fight. It's normal. But something seems off. It's only when the bartender returns with my drinks that I peel my gaze away from them.

"Thanks," I tell him.

Unable to resist, I glance in Vanessa's direction again, but she's gone.

VANESSA

I WALK OUT of the crowded bar and take a deep breath of the cool evening air. It's the end of August, and finally summer has begun to lose its grip on the weather. I'm a fall girl through and through.

I hoped Ryan wouldn't follow me, but he comes right out.

"So that's it? You're just going to walk away from me?" he says.

"That was the idea, but it seems you won't let me do that either."

"Excuse me for not wanting my girlfriend to spend the weekend in Vegas with a bunch of hos."

I whip my face to his. "Hos? So my cousins and my sister are whores to you?"

Ryan sneers, turning his beautiful-in-a-preppy-way face into an ugly mask. "I've seen the way they dress."

"Unbelievable. You know what, Ryan? I don't give a fuck what you think. We're done."

I stride away, fuming. I can't believe I wasted six months of my life with this asshole. That's what I get for breaking my rules about dating. I always swore I wouldn't date a frat boy because, in my book, they're all fuckers. Ryan proved me right.

"Don't you dare walk away from me."

"Watch me." Without looking back, I raise my hand and flip him off.

He drove, which sucks, but the bar isn't far from my place, so I'm fine with walking. I hear Ryan run after me, which I ignore. That is, until he grabs my arm and yanks me back.

"I told you not to walk away from me," he grits out.

"Let me go!" I try to break free from his grasp, but he sinks his fingers deeper into my arm.

"I don't think so, sugar. You see, *I'm* the one who decides when this relationship ends, and I'm not done with you yet."

He pulls me toward him, snaking his free arm around my waist, and then forces his mouth on me. I clamp my lips shut as I try to push him off. I can't budge him, and that makes me even madder. I'm not a helpless chick—I should be able to fight him off. He pushes me against the side of a random car and nudges my legs apart with one thigh. Fucking hell. Is he seriously assaulting me?

Adrenaline shoots through my veins. I refuse to be the victim. He's stronger than I am, so I use the only weapon at my disposal. My teeth. I bite his lower lip until I taste blood.

He pulls his head back, touching the cut. "You bit me," he says, as if he's surprised.

His body is still blocking me, but there's a gap between us now, so I use that to my advantage. I shove him back with my free hand, hoping he'll release me. No such luck. His eyes turn murderous, and in the next second, his hand is wrapped around my neck and he's choking me.

"You fucking bitch. Who do you think you are?"

"I may be a bitch, but not your bitch, asshole."

"We'll see about that." He squeezes my throat tighter, and then traps my arm between our bodies before he releases my wrist and thrusts his hand up my skirt.

Angry tears gather in my eyes. I can't scream, and I can't free my arm to punch the side of his face. His fingers are already inside of me, rough and invasive. But the most concerning part is that I can't breathe, and black dots are forming in my vision. He's going to kill me before he has the chance to rape me. Or maybe that's his goal—to fuck my corpse.

"Get off her!" someone yells.

Ryan is yanked back in the next second, and as I gasp for air, I see that my savior is none other than Paris.

Ryan staggers back and then tries to punch Paris, but he's no match for the Rebels' linebacker. Paris blocks his punch and delivers one of his own, sending Ryan to the ground.

"You asshole! You broke my nose," Ryan whines a moment later.

"Oh, I plan to break way more than that, motherfucker." He steps toward him, but I finally snap out of my paralysis and grab the back of Paris's jacket.

"No. He's not worth it." My voice sounds hoarse.

He looks over his shoulder, confusion etched on his face. "He assaulted you."

His words feel like a punch to my throat. I know what Ryan did, but hearing it out loud gives it more meaning, more weight.

"And he's going to get what he deserves, but not from you."

"Say goodbye to football, fucker. I'll make sure you never play again," Ryan retorts, already back on his feet.

The fact that he thinks he can issue threats after what he did to me makes my blood boil. I walk around Paris, and before Ryan knows what's coming for him, I kick his family jewels with all my strength.

He howls, bending forward while he cradles his junk. "You crazy bitch," he wheezes.

Paris gets between Ryan and me and asks, "Are you okay?"

"I'm shaken, but okay."

He keeps staring at me as if he wants to peer into my thoughts and check if I'm telling the truth. Finally, he asks, "Do you want to call the cops?"

I'm still riding the anger and adrenaline, yet the idea of rehashing what happened with a bunch of strangers makes me queasy. Hell, and what about my parents? If the police get involved, they'll know, and then my entire family will know. The story will follow me for the rest of my life. I'll cease to be Vanessa, the kickass soccer player, and become the Castro girl who was almost raped by her douche ex.

"No," I say. "Hopefully, I ended his ability to procreate tonight."

Paris narrows his eyes and clenches his jaw so hard, I can almost hear his teeth grinding together. He's judging my decision, like he always does. I shouldn't expect any less from him.

The sound of a car peeling out of the parking lot draws my attention to where Ryan had been a minute ago. The weasel took advantage of our moment of distraction and ran away.

Paris curses under his breath, aggravating me further.

"Why are you upset? I'm the one who was attacked."

He opens and shuts his mouth without saying a word, and then shakes his head. "I'm not upset, I'm angry as fuck."

"Me too." I cross my arms, feeling cold and vulnerable.

It seems the effects of the adrenaline are gone and the reality of what happened tonight has finally sunk in fully.

"I'll take you home," he says softly, which only makes matters worse.

I'm on the verge of crying now, but hell if I'll let the tears fall in front of him. He saved me from a horrible situation tonight, but that hasn't erased all the occasions he acted like a jerk toward me.

I follow him to his truck in silence, and the nonverbal streak continues all the way to my place. Only when he parks in front of my house does it dawn on me that I never gave him my address. I live near campus in a rental my parents got for Heather and me after our freshman year. Quite a few students rent in this neighborhood, but there are also young families. Our house isn't new, and we've had a few plumbing issues, but I love that the neighborhood is quiet and safe.

"How do you know where I live?"

"I've been here before."

My brows arch. "You have? When?"

"I don't know. Last year? Heather threw a party when you were at an away game."

That information should make me angry again. Heather never told me about any party. We have a deal that parties need to be agreed upon by both of us beforehand. But I've spent all my rage, and all that's left is sadness.

"Well, thanks for giving me a ride home." I reach for the door handle.

"Are you going to be okay? Is your sister home?"

"I don't think she's home, but I'll be fine," I lie.

Paris, being the nosy person he is, doesn't buy my bullshit. "I'll wait with you until she gets home. You shouldn't be alone."

I'd fight him, because he's not the boss of me, but the truth is, he's right. I could call Sadie, or any of my other teammates, but then I'd have to tell them what's wrong, and I don't want anyone to know. I suppose Paris will have to do.

"Okay. You can come in."

Tilting his head, he stares at me. "Good. I was expecting you to be difficult."

"No. I've run out of sass." I get out of the truck and don't wait for Paris to follow me.

By the time I reach the front door, tears are rolling down my cheeks, and I pray he doesn't see them.

7

PARIS

I ALMOST SAID the wrong thing to Vanessa back in that parking lot. I couldn't believe she didn't want to call the cops. But clarity came to me before I could put my foot in my mouth. Who am I to judge her decision in that situation? I'm glad she let me come into her house, but now I don't know what to do.

As soon as she opened the front door, she bolted down the hallway. I glance around, noticing that everything is immaculate and organized. Even the picture frames on the bookshelf are placed in chronological order. I spend some time looking at them, but when I see a picture of our old youth group at church, I have to look away. Cory and I are in that picture.

I wonder why it's on display and who put it there. Vanessa didn't seem to care much about my family back then. She never called or came to see me after Cory died. And then she acted surprised when I didn't want anything to do with her when we met again in high school.

I shake my head, refusing to dwell on the past, and make myself comfortable on her couch. But as much as I don't want to think about our younger years, I can't help it. I was a mess, and even if she didn't want to be my girlfriend, I could have used a friend.

Time slips by, and when I finally return to the present, I see that a half hour has passed and Vanessa is still in her room. I'm all for respecting people's privacy, but I'm worried sick she might do something foolish. I have to check on her.

Mind made up, I take a few steps toward the hall, but I freeze when I hear a door open at the end. I debate running back to the couch, but this house is too small, and she'd catch me. A few seconds later, she returns to the living area and finds me there, rooted to the spot like a damn tree.

Her eyes widen a fraction. "Were you coming to check on me?"

I rub the back of my neck. "Yeah."

"I had to take a very long shower."

It's then that I notice her hair is damp. I also see the red mark that asshole left on her neck. The anger from before returns with a vengeance. "Is your throat bothering you?"

She covers the mark with her hand. "A little."

"I can make you tea with honey." I veer for the open kitchen without waiting for her reply.

"It's my house, Paris."

I look over my shoulder and take note of her standing there, a frown on her face and her hands on her hips. Something stirs in my mind, and my pulse accelerates. It's an old memory of her, looking at me just like that before everything went to hell. Despite the current situation, I grin. That pissed-off look is better than the dead look in her eyes from before. "I know it's your house, but I want to help."

"Aren't you the gentleman?" She crosses her arms.

"Sarcasm noted. For your information, I *am* a gentleman."

She snorts. "I guess for a select few."

"Are you still mad about last semester's incident?"

"That's just your most recent offense. You took your girlfriend's side as usual, even though you knew she was being a fucking bitch."

I wince. Vanessa isn't wrong. I've acted like a total jerk many times because of Lydia.

"I'm sorry. I had my reasons. Besides, she's no longer my girlfriend. I thought you knew that."

She scoffs, rolling her eyes. "It took you long enough. I bet your teammates let out a collective sigh of relief."

She's not holding back, but everything coming out of her mouth is a reminder of the firecracker girl who stole my heart when I was thirteen. I smirk. "Andy set off fireworks to celebrate."

Surprisingly, she returns the grin. "That tracks."

We don't speak for a couple of beats. I don't know why she's staring at me in silence, but I know why I'm staring back. My heart is beating faster, the same way it did all those years ago when we were alone in the park and I confessed I liked her.

"You said you'd make tea?" she asks, breaking the spell.

I blink fast, and then look at everything but her. "Yeah. Just point me in the right direction."

She walks around me and proceeds to open cabinets. "Heather and I aren't huge tea drinkers, but I know I saw chamomile here somewhere."

After she empties most of the cupboard, she finally locates the tea box, which she sets on the counter next to two coffee mugs and a jar of honey.

"There. Now you have everything you need to make tea."

"Uh, where's your kettle?"

"Don't have one. Just stick the mug in the microwave." She's grinning when she heads to the living room. I suppose there isn't much to making tea, and she did half the job by getting the supplies ready.

Well, there's nothing for it but to make the tea.

Vanessa turns on the TV, and when I join her carrying two steamy cups of tea with honey, I see she has *The Fellowship of the Ring* on the wide screen.

"I didn't know you were a *Lord of the Rings* fan." I set one mug in front of her on the coffee table.

She pulls a pillow over her lap and crosses her legs. "I don't trust anyone who isn't a fan."

My lips twitch upward. "That's a good qualifier to judge one's character."

I bet that motherfucker ex of hers didn't like *Lord of the Rings*.

"Ryan hated it," she says as if reading my mind. "I should have dumped his sorry ass when I found out."

She reaches for her mug and blows on the liquid before taking a tentative sip.

"I never understood why you went out with that loser in the first place."

Her expression closes off. "You're one to talk."

"Touché. But in my defense, Lydia wasn't always difficult. I wouldn't have fallen in love with her otherwise."

I don't know why I said that to Vanessa. Maybe I'm trying to salvage my reputation for being such a pussy. I'm not even sure I ever truly loved Lydia. I try my tea, burning my tongue in the process. I should have blown on it first. I chance a peek at Vanessa, wondering if she noticed my grimace. Her gaze is glued to the TV screen, and her jaw is set in a hard line. Hell. I don't know what to make of that expression.

"What's wrong?"

"Nothing."

The sound of a key makes me sit up straighter. I turn my attention to the front door, belatedly remembering I don't have an excuse for being here with Vanessa. It's either the truth, or Heather will think we were about to hook up.

Vanessa's twin stops short when she finds me sitting like a damn statue on her couch. She cuts her eyes to Vanessa, and I can guess the direction of her thoughts.

"Hey. I thought you were going to stay at Ryan's tonight," she says.

"Change of plans," Vanessa replies curtly.

"Oh." She turns to me. "Are *you* spending the night, then?" I open my mouth to deny it, but Heather continues. "If you are, please make sure you lower the toilet seat after you use it."

"He's not spending the night, Heather," Vanessa grits out. "We're just watching a movie."

"Fine. Make sure you keep the volume low, please. I have to wake up early tomorrow for cheer practice." She strides down the hallway and a moment later, a door bangs shut.

"Do we have to worry about your sister spreading rumors about us?" I ask.

Vanessa looks at me. "Why, Paris? Are you afraid Lydia is going to find out and come after your balls?"

My nostrils flare, but I don't fall for her baiting. She's mad about something I said earlier. Maybe it was my comment about Lydia not being a bad girlfriend in the beginning. Whatever the reason, I have to maintain my cool. Vanessa just went through an ordeal no one should have to experience. If she wants to use me as her punching bag, so be it. I plan to stay until she kicks me out.

"No. I'm thinking about you."

"Right, because it's okay for guys to dump their girlfriends and jump in bed with another chick thirty seconds later. But if a girl does it, she's a whore."

"I don't make the rules."

"The rules are garbage. I'm sick and tired of the double standards."

Ah hell. I can't believe the conversation has devolved to this topic. This would be dangerous territory on any occasion, but with Vanessa ready to blow, it's definitely not a place I want to linger.

"That's why my favorite character in the *Lord of the Rings* franchise is Éowyn," I say, keeping my face glued to the TV.

I can sense Vanessa's gaze burning a hole through my face.

"For real?" she asks after a moment.

I look at her then. "For real."

She clamps her jaw while her sharp gaze remains glued to my face. Then, begrudgingly, she says, "Well, Paris. You're not a total lost cause."

I grin and face the TV again, trying to ignore how her comment lightened my heart.

8

VANESSA

I WAKE up with a beefy arm wrapped around me. My head is resting against the shoulder attached to said arm. Shit. Paris spent the night? The light coming from the partially closed shades tells me he did.

Careful not to wake him, I dislodge his arm and scooch to the side. We're still in the living room, wearing all our clothes. Relief washes over me. I didn't try to fix a mistake by making a bigger one.

Paris fidgets and then makes a sound in the back of his throat that's pure male. For a moment, I get carried away and imagine what it would be like waking up in his arms after I rode him to exhaustion. He's always been so handsome, but now, with all his muscles and insane tattoos, he just oozes sex appeal.

He opens his beautiful blue eyes then and catches me staring. Busted. Do I have a lust-infused gaze? Was I drooling? His first reaction is to reward me with a lazy smile that turns my insides into jelly. It's unfair how gorgeous he is even after sleeping on the couch in an awkward position. I probably look like a witch.

"Hey," he says in a rough voice that's seriously impairing my ability to think straight.

"You spent the night."

And just like that, the grin vanishes from his face, and he sits straighter on the couch. "Yeah. I'm sorry. I must have fallen asleep."

Ah hell. Me and my big mouth. "I didn't mean to accuse you of anything. It wasn't my intention." I spring to my feet. "Coffee?"

Paris follows my example, but heads for the door instead. "Nah. I'd better get going. I think I overstayed my welcome."

Disappointment floods through me, and I don't know why. I didn't even want Paris to come in last night. Why am I bummed out that he's leaving?

"Thanks for staying with me last night."

He turns, and a hint of a smile teases his lips. "You're welcome."

His hand reaches for the door handle, but he pauses and stares at it for a couple of beats. I hold my breath as hummingbirds flutter in my chest.

"Can I text you later?" he asks.

My heart skips a beat. Why am I reacting to Paris like I'm thirteen again?

"Sure. Do you have my number?"

He shoves one hand in a pocket, lowering the waistband of his jeans enough to reveal a patch of tanned, taut skin, and then pulls out his phone. My eyes zero in and remain glued to that peekaboo show for a second too long.

"Here. You can type it in."

I jerk my head up again, mortified that he caught me staring like an idiot twice in a row.

Our fingers brush in the exchange. I try not to think too much about it. *There were no electric sparks, Vanessa. It's all in your head.* Maybe this is a belated reaction to last night's ordeal. It cannot be lingering feelings from my stupid crush of nine years ago. My mind must need a distraction, and Paris Andino fits the bill.

My hands are shaking, though, as I type my digits into his phone. When I return the device to him, I do my best to not touch him again.

He types something before putting the phone away. "There. I sent you a text. Now you have my number too."

I'm curious to read his message, but I control my impulse to check. He finally opens the door, squinting as the morning sun hits his face.

"It's going to be another gorgeous day in Cali." He shields his eyes with his hand and glances at the sky. "Do you have any plans?"

Plans? I scramble my brain, trying to remember. I know something is going on today.

Paris laughs. "I just asked if you had plans, I didn't give you a math equation to solve."

"Why did you say that?"

"Your face..." He shakes his head. "Never mind. Don't worry. My question was innocent. No ulterior motives this time."

A blush spreads through my cheeks. I can't believe he just referred to our first-kiss moment.

He clears his throat. "Anyway, I'd better go. I'll check on you later."

I watch his wide, strong back as he walks to his truck, my brain working furiously in the background, trying to remember what I was supposed to do today. I'm drawing a blank. No surprise there. I'm operating without my caffeine fix.

My phone vibrates in my hand—it's a calendar reminder for a hair appointment.

"Fuck!" I run back to the house.

Now I remember my plans for today. My cousin Lorena's wedding. I can't believe I forgot. And now I have to deal with my family and pretend I wasn't almost raped in a parking lot by Ryan last night. Hell and damn.

PARIS

I WISH I didn't have to leave Vanessa's place in a hurry. Spending the night wasn't in the plan, and I have a million things to do before going to my folks' place later. The first is heading over to Andreas's place for another tasting fest. He decided to pursue a career in baking, and he loves to use us as his guinea pigs. Not that I'm complaining. He's a talented motherfucker.

I'm already late, but there's no way in hell I can show up at his apartment wearing the same clothes I wore yesterday. He'll demand to know where I spent the night—meaning, who I slept with—because besides being obsessed with cooking, he's also a fucking busybody. He loves to know all the juicy gossip so he can tease us to no end. And since he was firmly in the I-hate-Lydia camp, he's been trying to help me out in the romance—*hookup*—department.

The music on the radio gets cut off by an incoming call. I press the accept button right away. "Hey, Dad."

"Good morning, son. Where are you?"

"Uh, on my way home. Why?"

"Hold on." I hear the sound of his footsteps, and then the *snick* of a door shutting. "Lydia is downstairs with your mother. She's in tears."

"What? Why? What happened?" I fire off those questions

automatically, but then I remember she's no longer my girlfriend and I shouldn't let her theatrics control me anymore.

"Something to do with you ignoring her phone calls and not spending the night at your place."

My stomach coils tightly. How the hell does she know I was gone all night? She either waited for me outside my building like a psycho, or she cornered one of my roommates. Both are terrible scenarios.

"I'm ignoring her calls to send a message that we're over. I thought she was getting better."

"That girl has severe mental issues, son. I can't tell you enough how glad your mother and I are that you put an end to it. We never liked her."

That's total BS. They loved Lydia in the beginning, because she comes from a respectable family. I love my parents, but they put too much value on appearances and status. For instance, when they saw my first tat, my father yelled at me for hours and my mother didn't talk to me for weeks. *No patient will want to be operated on by a surgeon who looks like he belongs to a motorcycle club.* Those were my father's words.

They calmed down only when they saw that it was a tribute to Cory. They probably thought I wouldn't get more ink done. Now I'm covered in tattoos, and there's not a damn thing they can do about it.

"What do you want me to do about Lydia?"

"Your mother wants you to come over and deal with her."

The idea makes my skin crawl. If I show up now, I'll never make it to Andreas's place.

"Can't. I'm already late for an important appointment."

"She's your girlfriend, Paris," Dad replies, sounding frustrated.

"My ex-girlfriend," I retort. "You know what's going to happen if I cave to her emotional blackmail. She'll think she can get me back, and I can't return to that bullshit."

He sighs. "We definitely don't want to encourage her. I'll make up an excuse. Don't worry."

"Thanks, Dad."

"What's the appointment? If it's important, you shouldn't be late."

I groan in my head. I shouldn't have expected Dad to let that one slide. He's a stickler for rules and manners. People being late is one of his pet peeves, which is ironic, because he sometimes makes his patients wait for up to an hour before he sees them. In his mind, in-demand doctors shouldn't be readily available. If they're running on time, it means they aren't good.

His view of the world is seriously messed up.

"I'm meeting Coach Clarkson for breakfast," I lie. "If I hurry, I'll be there just in time."

He grumbles. "You definitely don't want to upset your coach. And you'd better be here on time. Only the bride is allowed to be late to a wedding."

Hell. I'd forgotten where I'm supposed to be later today.

"Do I really need to come to this thing?"

"Yes, Paris. You do. Especially after leaving your mother and I alone to deal with your crazy ex. I'll see you later."

He ends the call abruptly, something he always does when he's pissed. Shit. If going to a stupid wedding wasn't already bad enough, now I have to deal with my aggravated folks. It's going to be a hella fun party.

9

VANESSA

I THOUGHT today was going to be hard. I was never good at pretending, but it turns out, the chaos of being in the midst of a wedding party is exactly what my mind needed to not dwell in darkness. My family never met Ryan—today was going to be the day of formal introductions. But everyone is busy freaking out over nothing, so no one has asked me about him yet. It was providential that he decided to show his true colors before more damage was done.

Heather—bless her vanity—has been too preoccupied with her hair, makeup, and clothes to bother me. I'm sure eventually she's going to corner me and ask what Paris was doing in our house last night. Maybe I should tell her about Ryan. I know she won't tell a soul if I ask her to keep it a secret. But I'm not ready for that conversation yet.

"What are you doing sitting down, child?" Aunt Lorena marches in my direction, her arms moving wildly.

"I was resting my feet."

She grabs my arm and forces me to stand. "Your dress is all wrinkled now."

I step away from her and smooth the offending lines. "It's not."

"Amateur," Heather sighs from across the room.

She found a mirror and has been preening in front of it for God knows how long. She's only a bridesmaid. I can't imagine what it's going to be like when she's the bride. One word flashes in my mind. *Bridezilla.*

My cousin Lorena—yeah, she was named after her mom— finally makes her grand entrance into the room designated for her wedding party. I try to keep my face from showing how much I detest her dress. It's simple and, dare I say, prudish. If I ever get married—which I don't think is going to happen—I'd probably go for a modern style too, but what she's wearing is a snooze. I bet it cost a pretty penny, though.

I glance at Heather who, unlike me, is not hiding what she thinks. Her face is twisted into a scowl. I hurry to her side before the Lorenas can see her expression. If Mom finds out Heather was acting like... well, like Heather, she'd give us both an earful. In her infinite wisdom, Mom believes twin sisters are supposed to keep each other in line.

"Reset your face to factory settings, Heather," I tell her.

She blinks fast. "What?"

"You know, the usual resting bitch face."

My teasing does the trick. She focuses her displeasure on me. "You're hilarious, Vanessa."

"I know." I smirk.

"What do you want?"

I lean closer to whisper in her ear. "Your face showed how much you luuuve Lorena's dress. I came to run interference."

She rolls her eyes. "Thanks for the save."

"You're welcome."

She looks over her shoulder for a moment, and then it's her

turn to lean in. "You have to agree with me. She looks like shit. I wouldn't be caught dead wearing that nineteenth-century nightgown."

I fight the urge to laugh. "Well, maybe if you were a ghost, you'd wear it."

She wrinkles her nose. "Nuh-uh. If I ever come back to haunt you, I'll be wearing something glorious designed by Alexander McQueen."

"Why would you haunt *me*?"

"Because you're a pain in my ass."

"I'm deeply hurt." I fake a distraught expression and press my hand against my chest. "I'm pretty sure there are other people you could haunt instead. Maybe one of your ex-husbands, who you caught cheating on you with his secretary."

Instead of being offended by my remark, she smiles. "Yeah, I'd haunt his ass too."

"Girls, the ceremony is about to start." Mom waves maniacally at us. "Come on."

"Oh goody," I murmur.

As Lorena and Aunt Lorena leave the room, beckoning all of us to follow, Heather glances at my wrinkled dress. "Shit. Mom is gonna have a cow when she notices those lines."

"Well, go in front of me, then."

"It's not gonna work," Heather singsongs.

She does walk ahead of me though, and I stay glued to her back, but like an eagle, Mom manages to notice what I was trying to hide. She grabs my arm and forces me to stop.

"What did you do to your dress?"

"Nothing." I step back, running my hands over the skirt.

"She sat down," Heather, the traitor, replies.

Mom pinches the bridge of her nose. "*Meu Deus, joguei pedra na cruz.*"

Shit. She's speaking in Portuguese, which means she's pissed.

"No one told me I wasn't supposed to sit down."

"It's a taffeta dress, of course you can't sit down."

"Yeah, Vanessa. That's like Fashion 101," Heather chimes in.

I glare at her through narrowed eyes. It's a promise of retaliation, and she'd better believe it'll come sooner rather than later.

"Nothing to do about that now. Everyone is waiting," Mom replies.

She pushes me through the door, and we all go down the stairs of the Malibu megamansion Lorena's parents rented for the joyous occasion. I can't even begin to imagine how much it cost.

Aunt Lorena is pacing at the bottom, blowing smoke through her nose like she's Daenerys's dragon about to melt the Iron Throne. "What took you so long?" she asks. "Get outside and in line already."

Mom hurries out the door to find Dad in the family seating area at the head of the aisle, and Heather veers for her spot in the line. The processional music starts, and Aunt Lorena makes her entrance. Since I'm the last of the bridesmaids to walk down the aisle before the maid of honor, I don't go very far. Cousin Lorena gives me a death glare, as if I made her wait for hours and not a couple of minutes. With that sour puss, either she'll either make it rain on her wedding day, or the groom will run away.

A friend of Aunt Lorena who's acting like a glorified wedding planner shoves a small bouquet of flowers into my hands and practically pushes me forward when I don't start walking on my cue. Not expecting the "help" and unused to having my leg movements restricted, I stagger forward, almost losing my balance completely. That would have been a scene-stealing moment, to fall flat on my face just before the bride goes down the aisle.

I manage a save and regain my balance, but as I do so, my gaze darts to my right and collides with Paris's amused one.

You have got to be kidding me.

PARIS

AFTER BEING roped into coming to the wedding of someone I hardly know because my parents want to parade me around, I was prepared to be bored out of my mind. They love to boast that I play for the Rebels and I'm headed to med school next year, as if those are their accomplishments, not mine. Sure, they helped along the way by paying for all those football camps and extra classes. That doesn't make me feel any less like a show pony.

Thanks to the Lydia drama earlier, the possibility that Vanessa might be here wasn't on my radar. I didn't connect the dots until I saw her. The bride is her cousin, something I should have known, considering we used to attend the same church every Sunday until the great scandal of my thirteenth year—a.k.a. when Cory's friend stole Father Medina's wine.

Now I can't help the thrill of excitement that rushes through me as I watch her walk down the aisle, wearing a formfitting dress that accentuates all her assets. I drown out the rest of the circus, because my attention is now solely on the most beautiful bridesmaid I've ever seen. The lavender color of her dress looks great against her tanned skin. And I don't know what they did to her hair, but it looks luscious and soft. I'd give anything to run my hands through the strands.

She's always had a nice ass, but now... damn. The sight is giving me a boner, which is awfully inconvenient and inappropriate, considering my mother and father are sitting next to me. I need to stop imagining things that aren't going to happen. I adjust my pants and force my eyes away from Vanessa's curves. Mercifully, she finishes her walk fast, removing the temptation.

Perhaps I should pay attention to the ceremony.

I do try, but my eyes have a will of their own and keep wandering back to Vanessa. During one of those moments, she looks in my direction, as if sensing my stare. I should look away, pretend it isn't her I'm watching, but I hold her gaze instead. She's too far away, and I can't begin to guess what she's thinking.

I'm not sure what's happening to me. For the longest time, I was able to pretend I had moved on. Before I fell for her, she was one of my best friends, a constant in my life. We didn't go to the same middle school, but I used to see her every weekend at the country club and at church. So when I lost Cory and she vanished from my life, it was a blow I couldn't recover from. I held on to my rancor, shut her out, and allowed Lydia to feed my animosity toward her. Vanessa never explained why she didn't contact me after I lost my brother. Maybe I should have asked her.

The connection breaks when the priest declares the couple husband and wife. After the kiss, the crowd erupts into cheers and applause. The newly married couple walk down the aisle side by side, followed by their wedding party. Vanessa is the only one who doesn't follow the procession train. The groomsman she would have been paired with walks alone, looking confused.

I look for her, but she's gone. Everyone begins to stand up, and I follow suit. But as I move into the aisle, I can't help but look over my shoulder and search for her.

Damn it. Where did she go?

10

VANESSA

PARIS DIDN'T TAKE his eyes off me during the entire ceremony, and I want to know why. I can't believe Aunt Lorena invited the Andinos, knowing how my mother feels about them.

Actually, I can. Mom and Aunt Lorena are stepsisters and never truly got along. Their relationship makes mine with Heather look like rainbows and cupcakes. Heather gets on my nerves, and I get on hers, but that's mostly because we're super different. We aren't besties, but I know she has my back and I have hers.

Just as Lorena and her new husband—I already forgot his name, because I'm that bad at remembering details that don't interest me—are declared married, I notice Granduncle Walter looking a little pale. While everyone else pays attention to the newlyweds as they return down the aisle together, I check on him.

"*Tio*, are you okay?"

"*Que?*" he leans closer, cupping his right ear.

"I asked if you're okay," I shout.

"*Ta muito calor. Muito calor.*" He yanks at his tie, trying to loosen it as he complains about the heat.

It's not even that hot out here, but maybe he's taking some medication that makes him flush, or his jacket is too thick. It does look like it's made of a heavy material.

"I'll get you some water," I say, and receive a blank stare in return.

He understands and speaks perfect English, but I repeat it in Portuguese just the same, and then use a shortcut to get to the reception's nearest bar. When I'm halfway there, it occurs to me that I should have helped him into some shade. But I'm pretty sure if I return without the water, he's going to be unhappy, and he'll let me know it. He's famous for his sharp tongue. I hike up my skirt and quicken my steps. The heels of my sandals sink into the grass, making my progression slower than I would have liked. As long as I don't trip again, I'll be fine.

The bartender looks bored when I reach him, but his face splits into a fake smile a second later.

"Hi, can I get some water, please?" I ask.

"Of course."

I grab the water and thank him. Urgency makes me turn around too fast, and I end up colliding with the person who was right behind me.

"Oops. Sor—oh, it's you."

Paris was the solid chest I collided with, and now my face is in flames. He looks too damn fine in a suit.

"You sound disappointed," he says through a smirk.

"Just surprised."

"I thought you saw me earlier."

"I did." God, I'm wasting time making a fool of myself while Granduncle Walter is withering under the sun. "I'm sorry. I have to get this water back to my granduncle. He isn't feeling well."

In a flash, the mirth vanishes from Paris's eyes and his serious mode activates. "What's the matter with him?"

"I don't know. He was complaining about being too hot. He's probably just dehydrated, right?"

"Where is he?"

"He's sitting in the front row."

"Let's get back to him, then."

Unbidden, he laces his arm with mine and steers me back through the grass path. I'm not sure if he's doing it because he saw me walking with difficulty earlier or if there's another reason. All I know is that my heart is beating much faster now, and I'm too aware of the feel of his strong arm against mine. Mercifully, we find Granduncle Walter alive and well.

I uncap the bottle and hand it to him. "Here's your water, *tio* Walter."

"*Ah, muito obrigado, querida.*" He takes a few sips and then lets out a satisfied sigh. Then his sharp gaze takes in Paris standing next to me. "*E esse rapaz, quem é?*"

I open my mouth to translate, but Paris extends his hand. "I'm Paris Andino. Nice to meet you, sir."

A spark of recognition lights up his eyes as they shake hands. "Ah, you're Dr. Andino's kid."

"That's correct. Are you feeling better now?"

"Yes. Much better. But I could use some assistance getting back inside."

"Of course." Paris steps forward and helps Granduncle Walter from his chair.

Instead of taking my shortcut, he leads him down the aisle, leaving me no choice but to follow the duo. It's a short walk, but Paris maintains a slow pace. He seems content chatting with my granduncle, and I'm shocked that the old man is giving him the time of day. He's a grumpy son of a bitch.

Is there anyone in the universe who doesn't fall prey to Paris's charms?

I get my answer not much later. As Paris leads Granduncle Walter through the double doors of the beachfront mansion, Mom comes out of nowhere and stops me from following them.

"What were you doing with that Andino boy, Vanessa?"

I fight the urge to roll my eyes. Mom has never forgotten about the wine-and-kiss incident. After they busted us, there was a huge argument between my parents and Paris's folks, which resulted in a fallout. Soon after, the Andinos changed parishes.

"He's a guest here, Mom."

"So? Do you plan to socialize with every single person at the reception?"

"He goes to the same school I do, or have you forgotten? We run in the same circles."

Her spine goes taut. "I'd prefer if you didn't. That boy got you drunk and took advantage of you. God only knows what would have happened if we hadn't found you. I can't believe Lorena had the audacity to invite his family."

Myriad emotions rush through me, and I don't know which one is strongest. I'm angry at my mother for making a big deal about something that happened eons ago, and distraught thanks to the reminder that what she feared could happen then *did* actually happen yesterday—or almost did. And the boy she mistrusts so much is the one who saved me.

"I heard it was Vanessa who attacked Paris that day," Heather says as she joins us.

I'd tell her to suck a lemon, but her interruption is much appreciated.

Mom strikes faster than a cobra. "Those rumors were spread by that awful woman."

By *awful woman*, she means Mrs. Nora Andino, Paris's mother. It's been only an hour since this event started, and already the drama level is high. I need a drink stat if I hope to survive the rest of the day *and* evening.

Now that Mom is distracted by Heather, I slink away into the house and head to the busiest area inside, which, conveniently, is near one of the bars.

Unfortunately, my path gets blocked by another pissed-off parent—Paris's mother.

"Hello, Mrs. Andino. Long time no see," I say in a sugary tone.

Her eyes narrow as she gives me a head-to-toe appraising glance. "You haven't changed much, have you?"

I'm ninety-nine percent sure that was meant as an insult, but I play along. "I disagree. I'm taller, and now I have these." I grab my breasts, pushing them higher. It took a while, but I finally caught up with Heather in the curves department.

Mrs. Andino's eyes bug out before they narrow to slits. "Crass as always. And I'm the bad guy for telling everyone you weren't the victim."

Fuck. Why is everyone hell-bent on reminding me of that day? It rubs raw a wound that's still bleeding. I bet if she knew what happened last night, she'd blame me for that as well.

"A pleasure as always, Mrs. Andino." I walk around her, hating that my eyes are now burning. I'm not going to cry over her cheap insult.

The bar is busy, and I need more than a glass of wine to calm my nerves. I spy a waiter going to the kitchen, so I follow him. No one pays me any attention as I search for the stash of booze. I finally locate a closet where there are several cases of wine, whiskey, gin, and other spirits. Picking something strong would be the smart choice, but I don't want to get drunk too fast. I choose a red wine, glad it's one of those bottles with a twist cap.

I can't return to the party holding my prize, so I veer for the door that leads out the side of the house where several white catering vans are parked. I want solitude, so I keep walking until I find the gate that leads to the beach. Since high-heeled sandals and sand don't mesh well, I get rid of my shoes and leave them by the gate before continuing my trek.

The moment my bare feet touch the sand, a sense of peace washes over me. I take deep breaths and stare at the ocean. The feelings of impotence and unworthiness slowly leave my body. Can I spend the entire reception here?

I'm supposed to be taking official pictures right now, but fuck that. I don't want to capture how dreadful I feel for eternity. No one will care that I'm not in them anyway. I was never close to Lorena—I was asked to be in the wedding party only because they felt they had to include me as family. Lorena will probably be thankful I'm not in the pictures. Plus, I'm already considered the black sheep of the family—might as well live up to my reputation.

Before I take a sip of wine, I walk around a natural bend in the beach to where a tall stone wall conceals me from any wedding guest onlookers. Feeling dejected, I sit on a small boulder and unscrew the bottle cap. The first swig is a large one, but the next swallows are not even mouthfuls. Drinking the wine too fast would mean I'd have to get another bottle soon.

"Care for company?" Paris's smooth voice reaches me through the wind.

I glance at him, noticing he took off his shoes as well. His tie is gone, and the first two buttons of his shirt are unfastened.

"I'd ask how you found me, but it seems following my trail has become your specialty."

One corner of his lips twitches up. "I saw you take the stairs to the beach from my vantage point. Your granduncle is fine by the way."

The jerkface is trying to make me feel bad for not asking, so I shrug and pretend his comment doesn't bother me. "He's a tough one. I wasn't concerned."

"Sure, sure."

"We have a saying in Brazil—*vaso ruim não quebra*," I continue, and then take another sip.

"I suppose you're not going to translate that for me." He sits next to me on the boulder—uninvited—brushing his shoulder against mine.

"The literal translation is bad vase doesn't break, but the meaning is nasty people live long. I thought you spoke Portuguese, or at least understood it."

"What Walter said was easy enough to guess."

"Walter, is it?" I raise an eyebrow, giving him a side-glance. "I didn't know you were already buddies."

"What can I say? We clicked." He meets my stare, his blue eyes dancing with mirth.

I look away in a rush before I drown in them. Then I bring the bottle to my lips, wishing the alcohol would start working already and melt away this new tension caused by Paris's presence. I can't deal with all the emotions his nearness is stirring in me. It's clearer than ever that he is my weakness.

"Can I have some of that?" he asks.

"Sure." I pass the bottle to him without looking, and then force my eyes to stay focused on the waves crashing against the shore.

We remain quiet for a while, and because I'm wrestling with my heart, I don't ask for the wine back. That'd mean talking to Paris some more.

He breaks the silence. "I'm sorry if my mother said something that upset you."

"She didn't say anything she hasn't before." Since he forced me to talk, I reclaim the wine, and this time, I drink a big gulp.

"Easy. There's more where that came from."

Like the classy girl I'm not, I wipe my mouth with the back of my hand. "I don't want to go back too soon. In fact, I want to stay out here for as long as I can."

He doesn't offer a comment for a while, and I begin to relax. Or maybe it's the wine finally kicking in.

"I'm in awe that you're here to begin with," he murmurs.

"Why would you say that?" I snap. "Did you expect me to curl up into a ball and cry my eyes out instead?"

"I... well, no. But... are you okay?"

I turn so he can see my scowl, and I realize my mistake a second later when I'm blasted by his charged stare. There are so many emotions swimming in his gaze, I can't possibly decipher them.

"Yes," I hiss and jump to my feet to put much-needed distance between us.

"You don't need to pretend with me, Vanessa. I don't expect you to have gotten over what that motherfucker did that fast."

"Shut up, Paris. You know nothing about me."

He runs past me and blocks my way. "You're right, I don't. I'd like to change that though."

His confession feels like whiplash. I step back. "Why?"

He clenches his jaw, keeping his penetrating gaze locked with mine. It brings back memories I buried deep in my mind a long time ago. He looked like this when I finally saw him again a few months after Cory's death. We bumped into each other at the country club. His cold demeanor that day broke my heart, and that wasn't the only time he hurt me since then.

"You know what? Never mind." I whirl around and stride away, but I move too fast and don't watch my step. My right foot sinks into a hole, and I lose my balance and fall at an odd angle, getting red wine all over the front of my dress. Pain flares around my ankle, making me see stars. "Fuck!"

"Are you okay?" Paris crouches next to me, looking all worried and shit. Meanwhile, I'm trying not to cry.

"No," I whimper.

"Let me see your foot." He wraps his strong hands around

my calf and lifts my leg from the hole. I'd take pleasure in his touch if I wasn't in so much agony.

"How bad does it hurt?"

"Pretty fucking bad. God, I don't need this."

"It might not be as serious as you think. It's probably only a sprained ankle."

"A sprained ankle will keep me on the bench for too long."

He hooks his arm with mine and helps me up. "Come on. Let's get you back to the house. Can you walk?"

I try putting weight on my right foot and let out a pitiful cry. "No."

Before I can stop him, he sweeps me off my feet and into his arms. "Paris, put me down."

"You can't walk. It's better if you don't put weight on your foot before we know what's wrong. It could do more damage."

That thought alone stops any further protest I might have. I'm still cradling the wine bottle as we come into full view of anyone standing on the balcony. It's my luck that my parents are the ones who see me first.

"Vanessa!" Mom yells and then vanishes from my view.

She's probably running to meet us halfway.

Here we go again.

11

PARIS

"I'm sorry," I tell Vanessa as I walk back to the reception.

"For what? My bad luck?"

"If I hadn't followed you to the beach, you wouldn't have twisted your ankle, and we wouldn't be about to get yelled at for hours."

"That's true. And why the hell am I still holding on to this bottle of wine?"

"You didn't want to litter?" My reply is meant as a joke, but it doesn't remove the frown lines between her brows. "It won't be as bad as the first time. We're adults now."

She snorts. "Have you met my mother?"

No sooner does she speak than the woman in question arrives at the gate. "*Vanessa, minha filha. O que aconteceu? O que este moleque fez?*"

I'm completely lost as to what she's saying, but I don't miss the death glare she aims my way.

"It's nothing, Mom. I wasn't paying attention and twisted my ankle. Paris is just helping me get back to the house."

"What happened?" Vanessa's father joins the scene, looking more worried than angry.

I see more people coming down the stairs, and brace for the onslaught of angry Brazilians, talking a mile a minute. My hope is that my folks aren't aware of the commotion. They'd only add fuel to the fire, and we'd have a repeat of the stolen wine scene. And now I don't have Cory to help me out. A sharp pang flares up in my chest, but I don't have time to dwell on it, not when I have to explain myself to Vanessa's family.

"Paris thinks I might have sprained my ankle," Vanessa answers her father.

"What does he know?" her mom sneers. "He's not a doctor yet, is he?"

"I've seen my fair share of injuries, ma'am. But you're right, I'm not a doctor. We need to take Vanessa to the ER to get her ankle X-rayed."

"*We?*" Her voice rises to a shriek. "You've done enough."

Damn it. I misspoke, and that wasn't my intention. I don't know why I included myself in the trip to the hospital. I have no business going with Vanessa anywhere, even though I wouldn't mind tagging along to make sure she's all right.

"Will you quit, Mom? Paris is only helping. Now could you please move out of the way so we can get up the stairs? I'm not exactly a lightweight, you know?"

Her parents and other curious people who came to snoop move out of the way to allow me to pass. I take the steps two at a time, mainly to put distance between us and them fast.

"You weigh nothing by the way," I tell Vanessa.

"Now you're just showing off. I'm packed with muscle."

Her reply makes me chuckle, despite the situation. "Your sass is back. I hope that means your ankle isn't as painful as before."

"Nah, I'm finally drunk enough that I can't feel it as much. With my luck, I'm sure I got hurt terribly and I'll have to forget the entire soccer season."

"Stop being so pessimistic. I'm sure it's not too serious."

When I reach the landing, there's a small crowd waiting for us. I spot Heather front and center, sporting a smirk. She takes a sip of her champagne, unfazed that I'm carrying her sister. Jesus, doesn't she care to know what happened to Vanessa?

"Paris, what in the world?" Mom's shrill voice catches my attention.

Hell. So much for hoping my folks wouldn't notice the tumult.

"Your son once again tried to corrupt my daughter." Vanessa's mother joins the scene, and I get a flashback of their fight of nine years ago.

"My son did no such thing!" Mother's eyes bug out.

"Do you think they'll come to blows this time?" Vanessa whispers.

"Hopefully not."

Her mother and mine begin their back-and-forth argument. The mother of the bride joins them and tries in vain to calm them down, which incenses Vanessa's mother more. If they weren't arguing about us, I'd record the confrontation and post it all over the internet. This is gold. Not one of them is paying attention to us now.

"If I tell you I can sneak us out and take you to the hospital, would you let me?"

"Do you see an opening for a swift escape?" Her eyebrows arch.

I mince to the side until we're not in the center of the circle, but we still have to get away without anyone noticing.

Heather appears out of nowhere. "Do you plan on carrying my sister for the entire reception, Andino?"

"She can't walk," I retort.

"Yes, Heather. I twisted my ankle, thanks for asking."

"Sure, and neither of you dislikes this arrangement." She finishes her drink and walks away.

Shit. Am I that transparent? But more important, why did she add Vanessa to her statement?

"Your sister is a piece of work," I mutter.

"Ignore her. I do most of the time. If you want to get out of here, it has to be now. Sooner rather than later our parents will notice we're not watching their shit show, and they'll come looking for us. I really don't want to deal with more yelling today."

I look over the heads of a few guests trying to stay clear of the argument. I don't mind having to special-order my shoes because of my size when I can see over any crowd. Being tall definitely has more perks than hindrances, and being able to find an escape route right now is one of them.

"I think I got it."

I make my move, striding away from the reception area via the path that leads to the side of the house. Soon I see all the white vans parked there, but most importantly, no guests.

"Did you drive?" she asks.

"Yeah. I don't attend events with my folks anymore without having a way to fly the coop."

"Smart. Unfortunately, I didn't have a choice about coming with my parents today."

"It's okay. I got you."

Surprisingly, she rests her cheek against my chest, making me feel all kinds of crazy shit. The scent of vanilla reaches my nose, igniting a little fire in the pit of my stomach. It's an aroma that's embedded in my memory. She must still use the same brand of shampoo as she did nine years ago. My heartbeat accelerates to a hundred, and the desire to hug her tighter is almost overwhelming. It seems all the emotions I suppressed when I was barely a teen are coming back to the surface like a volcanic eruption.

"Thanks, Andino. I almost don't mind that you're the reason I need to go to the ER."

There's no accusation in her tone. She must be buzzing.

"Hey, now. Your clumsiness is what caused your accident. Don't go spreading rumors." I stop next to the passenger side of my truck. "Can you stand for a second? I need to open the door for you."

"Yep."

I let her slide out of my arms. She braces a hand against the truck, standing on one foot. That's when I notice she isn't wearing her sandals.

"Shit, we forgot your shoes," I say.

She drops her gaze to the ground. "You too, buddy."

I look down as well, and then shrug. "It's okay. I can get them later. Besides, I have a pair of sneakers in the truck."

"Are you going to open the door for me, or are we waiting to get busted?"

"Oops, sorry."

When I unlock the door, the truck alarm beeps, making me wince a little. It's paranoia. No way anyone can hear it from the house.

I attempt to help Vanessa slide into the truck, but she puts her arm up. "It's okay, Paris. I got it."

She sets the almost empty bottle of wine in front of her seat and turns, facing me. Then she braces her hands against the doorframe, bending her knee in preparation for a little jump. Yeah, not gonna happen.

"Nope." I wrap my hands around her tiny waist and lift her onto the seat without effort. "There."

She watches me through narrowed eyes. "I could have gotten in without your help."

"I'm sure you could, and it'd probably have been pretty

entertaining to watch, but we're trying to get out of here in a hurry, remember?"

I can see her mind working to come up with a clever retort, but in the end, she simply swings her legs into the cab and shuts the door. I run around the front and, when I get behind the steering wheel, she's sporting a frown and her arms are crossed. Man, I wish I had the ability to read her thoughts. I could ask, and I plan to, but first, I need to get us out of here.

It's not prudent to drive without shoes on, so I twist my body to reach behind my seat. I know I threw a pair of sneakers somewhere in the back.

"What are you doing? I thought you were in a hurry to leave."

My fingers brush against one shoe. I snatch it and show it to her. "Looking for the other one."

"Ew, gross. Get that away from me." She pushes my arm back.

Ignoring her, I resume my search, but my movements are constricted thanks to the suit jacket. I dive farther between our seats and finally get a visual of the missing shoe. Stretching my arm to the max, I manage to grab it, but the noise of tearing fabric follows.

"You just ripped your jacket," Vanessa tells me.

"Noticed it." I return to my seat and, grumpily, put the shoes on, wincing that I didn't have the foresight to wipe off the sand first.

"You don't need to bite my head off."

"I didn't. You'd know if I did."

Annoyed, I put the truck in drive and head out of the parking area slowly to avoid making more noise than needed.

She snorts. "I think I can tell when you're being a jerk. Been there, done that."

My cheeks hollow as I work my jaw. A retort is on the tip of my tongue, but I can't fault her for that jab.

"Are you going to be mad at me the entire trip to the hospital?" I ask instead.

"Yes."

"I just wanted to help."

"I know. It's your knight-in-shining-armor complex at work."

I hold the steering wheel tighter. "I don't have a knight-in-shining-armor complex. But if I see a friend struggling, of course I'm going to help."

"So we're friends now?" I feel her stare on my face.

Curious, I peel my gaze off the road for a second to look at her. The distrust shining in her eyes kills me.

"For my part," I reply, wondering if she'll get the reference.

She blinks fast, and then faces the road. "Nice one, Frodo."

A smile tugs at the corners of my mouth, making me forget my ripped jacket and the family feud we probably reignited today.

12

VANESSA

As Paris guessed, I have a sprained ankle, and I have to wear a brace until the Ravens' trainer checks me and gives her diagnosis Monday morning. I called Coach Lauda on the way home to get it over with, thinking she'd be mad as hell. She was only concerned about my well-being, which surprised me. I'm feeling dejected just the same. My shoulders slump as I stare at my phone.

"What's wrong?" Paris asks.

"I'm not sure. I thought I was gonna get my ass chewed by Coach Lauda."

"Why would you think that? What happened was an accident."

I shrug. "I don't know. Maybe because I know it could have been avoided. If I hadn't been drinking, and if I hadn't let you get under my skin, I'd have seen the hole in the sand."

"I got under your skin?"

Shit. I can't believe I let that confession roll off my tongue.

I let out an exasperated sigh and look out the window. "Yes, Paris. You did. Are you happy now?"

His calloused hand covers mine and squeezes, sending a zing of pleasure up my arm. My heart takes off, chasing the butterflies that spring from my stomach. I glance at him, nervous all of a sudden.

"I'd be happier if you'd forgive me for all the crappy stuff I did to you in the past," he says.

A huge lump gets lodged in my throat. I want to believe him so badly, but can I? There were many occasions where Paris acted like a jerk, especially throughout high school.

Unbidden, the prom night humiliation scene comes to the forefront of my mind. Paris and I were elected prom king and queen, but when it came to the official dance, he left me standing alone in the middle of the ballroom like an idiot and danced with Lydia instead.

"The list is a mile long."

He quirks an eyebrow. "Only a mile? I can deal with that."

My heart skips a beat. Damn it. I won't be able to keep my crush hidden if he keeps slinging his charm my way. Is that his intention? No, he's probably trying to clear his guilty conscience. That's all.

I realize I've been staring for far too long without saying a word.

My phone's ringtone breaks the spell. Unfortunately, it's my mother calling again. I've ignored her calls since we escaped the wedding, texting her only to let the family know I was on the way to the ER, but I didn't say which one.

"Are you going to keep blowing off your folks? It's only gonna get worse."

"I know, but if I tell them I'm home, they'll come running, and all I want to do right now is take a nap." I reach for the door handle, ready to hop out of his truck. We've been parked in front of my house a while now and there's no need to prolong the awkwardness.

"Hold on. I'll help you." He's out of the truck before I can protest.

My rebellious side wants to jump out before he has the chance to walk around the vehicle, but my stupid heart is looking forward to Paris's help. I want his hands on my body again. They felt too damn good. Man, I'm in trouble. I can't allow him to linger, or I'll end up doing something regrettable.

I do open the door myself and swing my legs to the side of the seat. He steps forward but stops suddenly, frowning.

"What's wrong? I don't think I gained a hundred pounds on the ride from the hospital. You can still lift me as if I weigh nothing."

With a shake of his head, he replies, "I... that's not it. I don't want to be handsy like before. It wasn't cool."

I roll my eyes. "For fuck's sake, Paris. I know you didn't mean anything dirty by it."

I wholeheartedly believe my statement until I catch a flash of guilt in his eyes. Maybe his mind was in the gutter when he touched me. Now I really want him to touch me again. I'm actually dying for him to pick me up caveman style. I can't even blame my crazy thoughts on painkillers, since I refused them. Maybe I'm still drunk.

"Do you want me to carry you to the front door?" he asks.

"Sure, if you don't mind."

And I'm in his arms again. Anyone seeing us wearing our fine clothing would think we're newlyweds. A bubble of laughter goes up my throat.

"What's so funny?"

I shake my head. "Nothing."

"Come on, Vanessa. You're going to make me self-conscious. Am I not carrying you right?"

"You're fine. Let me get the key from my bag. You can put me down."

He does so and waits nearby while I fish the small object from my tiny purse. I'm glad I kept it with me when I decided to hide from everyone at the beach.

"Do you want to come in?" I ask as I open the door.

"I thought you wanted to take a nap."

Damn it. He caught me.

"I do, but... I don't know. I think I should offer you a beverage for your troubles."

He narrows his eyes. "I will come in on the condition you tell me what you were laughing about."

"Oh my god, Paris. Why do you care?"

"My pride is at stake here. Laughter is not what I expect when I'm carrying beautiful women in my arms."

My heart swells and then shrivels. He thinks I'm beautiful, and yet jealousy pierces my chest, even though the upturn of his lips tells me he's joking. Why did he have to use the word in plural? I hop on one foot into the house, leaving the door wide open for him to follow. I must look ridiculous, but they didn't have crutches for me at the hospital. I need to get some tomorrow.

"It's silly," I say, and wait until he closes the door behind him to continue. "It just occurred to me that we looked like we just got married."

I didn't expect the confession to bring a blush to my cheeks, but here we are. I'm glad that I don't turn red like Heather does. Yippee-ki-yay for my tanned skin.

Paris chuckles. "What kind of ceremony did we have that I ended up with a ripped jacket and you have red wine stains all over your dress?"

"Uh, the fun kind?" I smirk.

His face splits into a radiant grin, and I neglect to breathe. I forgot how beautiful he is when he smiles.

"You're right. You *are* a silly girl. But it's good to hear your laughter. I've missed it."

Okay, now I forget how to do *all* the basic stuff. I don't move, I don't blink, I just stare at him like an idiot. Finally, I croak, "You've missed my laughter?"

He maintains my stare, and the intensity in his gaze turns up several notches. "I've missed you, Vanessa."

"I... I don't know what to say."

And clearly that isn't what he was expecting to hear, judging by how his face seems to crumble.

"It's okay, you don't have to say anything. I just wanted you to know." He glances at the kitchen. "How about that beverage?"

I swallow the lemon-sized lump in my throat and say, "Make yourself at home. I have to sit down." I head for the couch and plop there. Ideally, I should get out of this binding dress, but I don't want to leave his company just yet.

"Do you want anything? Tea with honey again?" he asks.

"God no. I need something stronger, please. There's tequila in the cupboard above the sink."

"Can you handle the burn?"

I give him a droll look. "I've drunk tequila before, Paris."

"I know, what I meant was..." He shakes his head. "Jesus, why can't I get my thoughts straight when I'm around you?"

"Uh, that sounds like a trick question."

"I never asked you how your throat was. It seems you didn't bruise after all."

Oh, and here I thought there was more to his statement. I touch my neck. "The wonders of makeup."

Instead of veering into the kitchen, he sits next to me on the couch. "How bad is it?"

Now it's my turn to get my thoughts in a jam. His nearness is doing in my head. "I... not that bad."

"If you hadn't stopped me last night, I would have bashed his face in with my fists."

"I know. That's precisely why I stopped you. He's not worth getting arrested. He's a weasel, a vermin who doesn't deserve the air he breathes."

I can't believe I let Ryan fool me with his good-guy persona. My ego was bruised, and I needed someone who treated me well, which Ryan did in the beginning. Then his true colors started to show.

Paris nods, then gets up. "So, let's have some tequila."

"Are you drinking too?" My eyebrows arch.

"One shot won't hinder me."

"Well, you can always stay." Holy shit. Did I seriously say that out loud? "I mean, on the couch like last night."

He laughs. "I got your meaning the first time. I think you're trying to use me as a buffer against your parents."

Relief washes over me that his train of thought went in that direction. "You wouldn't be a buffer—on the contrary. You'd be gasoline poured over fire."

"True."

I watch him grab the tequila and then get out two shot glasses without having to look for them. I wonder for a moment how he guessed their location. Maybe he already knows where we keep them from the last time he was here, partying with my sister. I'm not bitter *at all* about that. I wonder if he brought his bitchy ex with him. They were still dating at the time, so there's a high chance that he did.

He returns to my side and fills up the glasses. Then he hands me one and lifts his for a toast. "To your speedy recovery."

"*Tim tim,*" I reply in the Brazilian way, then I toss my head back and swallow the shot.

It burns down my throat in a good way.

Paris shakes his head and shudders. "I haven't had tequila in ages."

"You could have grabbed lemon and salt."

"Nah, that's for amateurs." He picks up the bottle. "Another?"

"Yes, please." He fills my glass again, but his own remains empty. "So, I'm to drink alone from now on?"

Looking sheepish, he rubs the back of his neck. "As much as I'd love to keep drinking, I can't. I have to drive home eventually."

"Right." I gulp the second shot, slam the glass onto the table, and melt against the back of the couch. My body is tingling and as light as a feather. I'm getting a good buzz.

"You look tired. Maybe I should go."

I grab his arm without thinking. "Don't go just yet."

His gaze bounces between my eyes as if he's searching for something. I don't know if he'll find what he's looking for in them, but I'm certainly getting pulled into his orbit. I lean forward, dropping my own gaze to his full lips, which are partially open.

"Vanessa..." He says my name like a caress.

I press a hand to his chest, loving how warm his skin is under his shirt. "Your heart is beating so fast."

He cups my cheek and rubs his thumb over my lower lip. "I know."

Our mouths are getting closer and closer... we're seconds away from making that regrettable mistake I shouldn't want, but really do.

The sound of a key turning pulls Paris away from me as if he was yanked backward by an elastic band stretched to the max. He jumps off the couch just as Heather walks in.

Fucking great.

"So, you're home already. Thanks for letting us know." She bangs the door shut and trudges into the kitchen.

"I *just* got home," I say.

"If you don't call Mom, she's gonna have an aneurysm."

"I will."

"I should go," Paris announces

I want him to stay, but now that Heather's home, it's better if he leaves.

"Yeah, you definitely should," she pipes up. "If you want to keep your nut sack attached to the rest of your body."

"What the hell, Heather!"

She gives an *I'm just telling the truth* shrug before she uncaps the water bottle she got from the fridge. "Mom is convinced Paris is up to no good. *Again.*"

If a person could die of embarrassment, I'd be in extreme danger of biting the dust.

"Message received," Paris replies. He glances at me. "I'll text you tomorrow, okay?"

"Yeah, sure. Drive safe. And thanks for the ride."

"Anytime."

No sooner does he walk out the door than Heather takes his place on the couch. "All right. I could have bought that you were just hanging out last night, but after today, that excuse won't fly anymore. What the hell is going on with you and Paris?"

"Nothing."

"Bullshit."

"I'm not lying!" I grab a pillow and hug it to my chest. My pitiful shield against my sister's inquisition. "And you'd better not start spreading rumors about us."

She gets up in a huff. "Please. With the way you two are behaving around each other, I won't need to say a word. The rumor mill will turn into a damn factory."

13

PARIS

LIKE AN IDIOT, I blew up Vanessa's phone yesterday, so it's no surprise that she ignored me save for the first reply. Maybe it's better if I let her be. We almost kissed after the wedding, and she's not someone I can simply make out with and move on. She has a hold on me whether I want it or not, and if I'm to stay away from complicated relationships from now on, I have to keep my distance from her.

School and football, those are the only two things I'll focus on. It's a good thing the season is starting this weekend with our kickoff game, and my classes this semester are extreme. Whenever I'm not practicing, my ass will be glued to a chair in the library.

As I walk to my next lecture, my head is pounding with the amount of information the biochemistry professor dumped on us this morning. I have ten minutes to spare, but the building for my next class is on the opposite side of campus, which means I have to haul ass if I'm gonna make it there on time.

A vibration in my pocket alerts me to a text message. It's fucking stupid that my heart lurches with the possibility that Vanessa might have texted me back. I fight the urge to check but lose the battle pretty quickly. To my disappointment, it's a stupid joke Puck, the goofball on our team, sent to the Rebels group chat.

"Paris!" a female voice yells from behind me.

I grind my teeth. I should have known Lydia would corner me at some point during this week. I was hoping it would take her longer to track me down. I put on my headphones and pretend I don't hear her as I keep walking toward my next class.

Something yanks on my backpack to make me stop.

Annoyed, I pull my headphones off and turn to...yep. Lydia. "What the hell!"

"You wouldn't stop," she replies, out of breath.

"Maybe because I didn't hear you."

"You've been avoiding me."

Ah, straight to the point. She was never one to beat around the bush.

"I've been busy." I move to keep walking, but she blocks my path.

"You said we could be friends. Was it all bullshit?" Her eyes fill with tears, a move I fell for so many times before, it's not even funny.

"What was so important that you had to go see my folks, Lydia?"

She bites her lower lip and drops her gaze to her shoes. "I needed you. I've been so lonely lately, and I have no one to talk to. You're the only person who gets me, Paris."

"I'm sorry, Lydia. I can't be your go-to person anymore."

She whips her face up to mine, her eyes now flashing with anger. "So that's it? Our years together mean nothing to you anymore. All the times I was there for you when you needed it most, forgotten."

Her raised voice starts to draw attention. *Great.* She's causing a scene again, and worse, she's going to make me late for class.

I lift my hand. "Stop right there. This is not going to work anymore."

"This what?" she shrieks.

"The guilt trip. I haven't forgotten the time we were together or how you helped me in my darkest hour, but it's in the past, Lydia. You have to move on. We both do. We're not good for each other."

Her hands ball into fists and her body is shaking now. *Hell.* I thought we were past this. It's been six months since we broke up. She's been to therapy, went to the fucking retreat in Colorado, but she's regressed to the same state she was in when I ended things.

A small crowd has gathered around us, and sadly some of the vultures are recording the scene. I need to end this before it gets worse. From the corner of my eye, a pair of crutches catches my attention. I turn, my stomach falling through the earth when I see Vanessa standing there. *Fuck.* That's the one witness I don't need.

I must have stared at her for too long, because Lydia sneers. "Oh, I get it now. *You* have moved on."

I return my attention to her, trying to hide the truth. "What are you talking about?"

"You're such a jerk. She's the reason you broke up with me, isn't she? That fucking Raven whore!"

Anger rises in the pit of my stomach. Lydia can call me names all she wants, but I won't tolerate insults toward Vanessa. Not anymore.

"Enough, Lydia," I grit out. "We're done here."

I walk away before I say something I'll regret. As I do, I glance around. Vanessa is no longer in the crowd, but I wonder if she stayed long enough to hear Lydia's insult.

A nimrod is still pointing his stupid camera at me, so I push his phone down none too gently as I walk past him. "Show's over, jackass."

Once I break through the ring of people, I search for Vanessa. She shouldn't have gotten far on crutches. Apparently she did, though, because I don't see her anywhere.

My phone pings again, but I ignore it this time. There's zero chance it's a text from her, and I have no fucks to give about anyone else.

VANESSA

"God, that wasn't pleasant, was it?" Sadie pipes up on the way to the humanities building.

"No," I grumble.

"I thought Paris broke up with that hag ages ago."

"He did. Six months ago."

"Blimey. Poor lad. It was painful to watch, but I couldn't look away."

"Yeah, she's a train wreck." I stop in front of the door, and since I don't see a button to open it, I ask, "Do you mind getting that?"

"Duh, obviously. Man, I'm gutted about your injury."

"It's okay. The trainer said I can return to practice in a couple of weeks. It sucks that I can't play for our first game though."

I'm glad we changed the subject, despite the new topic being my inability to play soccer for a while. I so didn't want to keep talking about Paris. Yesterday, I had a moment of clarity. As much as I'm into Paris, I can't allow myself to follow that path. It'll only lead to heartache and stress. So I replied to one of his texts to avoid being a total cow, but I ignored the rest. Witnessing his argument with his ex just served to reinforce my decision.

"That's brilliant! God, who do you think Coach Lauda is going to sub in your place?"

"I'm not sure," I reply absentmindedly. "Ginny Sanders maybe." Then I notice who is walking down the corridor toward us and freeze.

Ryan.

"Oh, your boyfriend is coming."

Shit. I never told anyone I broke up with him. Last weekend felt like I was caught in a tornado, like Dorothy in the *Wizard of Oz*. If I landed in Oz, then Lydia is definitely the Wicked Witch of the West. But who the fuck is Ryan in this scenario? I can't think of a character evil enough to represent him.

"He's *not* my boyfriend anymore," I reply through clenched teeth while my fingers curl tighter around my crutches.

Sadie doesn't have a chance to get another word in before the asshole is standing in front of us. My only solace is that Paris's handiwork still shows on Ryan's face.

"Good morning, ladies." He smiles despite his busted nose.

"What happened to your face?" Sadie asks, erasing the son of a bitch's smirk in a flash. God, I love her bluntness.

"Nothing. What happened to your friend?" He nods toward my crutches.

"Why do you care?" I snap. "Run along, Ryan."

He sneers. "I hope it's broken. It's exactly what you deserve."

Sadie jumps in front of me, body poised to strike. "What the fuck did you just say to her?"

Ignoring her aggressive stance, he walks backward with the odious smirk in place, the venom in his eyes aimed solely at me. "Karma is a bitch, babe."

Sadie makes a motion to go after him, but I use one of my

crutches to stop her. "Don't. He just wants to get a reaction from me. He didn't take the breakup well."

"That's no excuse. He acted like a total wanker."

"He *is* a wanker."

She glances at me. "When did you end things?"

"Last Friday."

Her eyes widen. "And you didn't tell me?"

Guilt sneaks its way into my heart. I could have told her that I had broken up with the douche without giving her all the nasty details.

"I'm sorry. I had a busy weekend with my family, and then the accident. It slipped my mind."

Pouting, she crosses her arms. "I'm still mad at you. I tell you everything."

"I know. I feel awful now that I didn't update anyone about my new single status."

Her expression softens. "You don't need to feel bad. And if I'm totally honest, I'm relieved you tossed that bellend to the curb. I never liked him."

I stare into the distance, thinking about what led me to start dating Ryan in the first place.

"Yeah, he was a bad decision. Proof that you shouldn't jump into a relationship as an attempt to mend a broken heart."

"Wait—what? Who's the arsehole I need to punch for breaking your heart?"

I blink fast, regretting my confession. "No one you know."

She narrows her eyes, and I can tell she's trying to see if I'm lying. "Lucky him then."

I give her a pitiful smile. "Come on. Let's get to class."

14

PARIS

I SHOULD TAKE the hint that Vanessa doesn't want anything to do with me. And after the scene she witnessed earlier today, I can't fault her for her decision. I spend the entire day trying to get my mind off her, but nothing works.

During practice, I play like shit. My concentration is shot. I get chewed out by Coach Harrison *and* Coach Clarkson. I can't blame them. We're playing our biggest rival this weekend, and we need a sharp defense.

In the locker room, Danny finds me. "Is everything okay with you, man?"

I stuff things in my duffel bag, avoiding eye contact. "Yeah, I'm fine."

He rests his foot on the bench next to my bag and leans forward. "Bullshit. Don't lie to me, Andino."

Damn it. He's not going to let this go. I raise my head to look at him. "I have personal shit going on. But I'm working on it."

"Are you referring to the argument you had earlier with Lydia?"

I straighten my spine, annoyed that the story has gotten around. "How did you hear about it?"

His cheeks hollow before he replies, "Sadie told me."

"Wait, who told *her*?"

"She saw you guys."

Shit. I only had eyes for Vanessa and didn't even notice the blonde firecracker standing next to her.

"Well, it wasn't pleasant, but that's not my only problem."

He claps my shoulder. "Do you want to have a drink after this so you can fill me in?"

"I appreciate the offer, but I can't tonight. I'm heading to the library to study."

"All right, but the offer stands if you change your mind."

"Thanks, bro."

In hindsight, maybe I should have accepted Danny's offer instead of keeping my original plan. But then again, he has a reputation for playing matchmaker. If he gets a whiff of my interest in Vanessa, I'm doomed. I should be thankful Andreas graduated already and they can't gang up on me.

I grab something from a vending machine and head to the main library. I see some familiar faces—mostly people in the premed program. I stand out in the library, not only because of my size, but because this isn't a place jocks typically hang out.

I head for my usual spot, a table in a corner by a large window, but it's occupied by none other than Vanessa. Electric surprise rushes through me. I quicken my steps until I'm standing right in front of her.

"I never pegged you as a library type of girl," I say.

She glances up from the old book she has in front of her, eyes round. "What are you doing here?"

I chuckle. "I'm a regular. I usually sit at this table."

"Oh. I didn't realize they were reserved. I'll leave." She begins to collect her things.

"I'm not asking you to go. It's big enough for both of us. We can share."

She stares at me like a deer in headlights. "I... well, as long as we don't distract each other. I really need to study."

I pull up the chair across from her. "Yeah, same here. What's your major? I don't think I've ever asked."

Her brows furrow. "How could you, when the only times you've spoken to me in the last nine years have been to antagonize me?"

Shame makes my face hot. I do feel horrible about the way I behaved, even though I believed I was right to act in that manner. I don't think that anymore.

"Psychology," she replies.

"Oh," I blurt out. I don't know why her answer surprises me.

"What? Don't tell me you disagree with that choice."

"No, of course not. I was just caught by surprise. I thought you wanted to play soccer professionally."

"That would be cool, but I still need to graduate with a degree, and psychology has always interested me."

I nod. "It's a good career path."

Still watching me, she taps her pen nervously against her notebook.

"What's wrong?" I ask.

She shakes her head and returns her attention to the old tome in front of her. "Nothing."

Despite almost messing things up, I'm smiling like an idiot as I pull out my laptop and log on to the school's website. I manage to keep my mouth shut for maybe a minute before I ask, "What class are you studying for?"

"Oh, medieval literature. It's an elective."

"Yikes, that sounds... brutal."

"Yeah, I'm regretting my life choices right now."

I can't help but think her statement has a double meaning. I should leave things well alone. I did promise I wouldn't distract her, but I'm too fucking curious.

"That asshole's not bothering you, is he?"

Her eyebrows shoot to the heavens. "Uh...no."

I sense the lie as soon as it rolls off her tongue. I know her too well. "He came looking for you today, didn't he?"

She leans back and crosses her arms. "We bumped into each other. It seems neither of us can shake off our past so easily."

I mimic her stance. "No, it seems we can't. But I won't let the past dictate my future."

"Me neither."

"Are you sure about that?" I raise an eyebrow.

"What do you mean?"

"Why did you ignore my texts, Vanessa?"

Man, I'm acting like a total creeper by putting her on the spot like this.

She opens and shuts her mouth, but no answer comes forth. To save the situation, I continue. "I just wanted to make sure your mother isn't distributing Wanted, Dead or Alive posters with my face on them."

My ruse works. She cracks a smile.

"No posters yet. But you never know with her."

"I'll give her a wide berth, then."

I force my eyes away from her gorgeous face and try to focus on the words in front of me. It takes me a while, but eventually, I get absorbed by the assignment and almost forget I'm sitting across from the girl of my dreams.

The moment the idea crosses my mind, I stop typing. I never thought about her in those terms. I had a major crush on her when we were younger, but I guess I was too immature to think like that. I glance at her again and immediately become ensnared by the way her luscious dark hair falls across her cheek, and how the soft light from the desk lamp turns her skin golden. She looks like a sun goddess, and I want to worship her.

She lifts her eyes, catching me staring. "What?"

"Nothing."

"Hmm, okay." Her stomach grumbles, and she makes a face. "Sorry about that. I forgot to eat before coming here."

I give her one of the snack bars I got earlier. "Here."

She looks around in a cagey manner. "I thought we weren't allowed to eat in the library."

"You can if you're sneaky about it."

Her luscious lips split into a grin before she snatches the snack from my hand. "Look at you, still breaking all the rules."

"Some rules are meant to be broken."

She nods and then attacks the food. I should look away, but my gaze drops to her lips and stays glued there long enough that she notices.

"Whuh?" she asks with her mouth full.

"You have crumbs all over your face."

She swallows and wipes the corners of her mouth. "Are they gone?"

"You missed some." I reach over and rub a spot under her lower lip.

She lets out a soft gasp and leans back a little. An apology is at the tip of my tongue, but when I see how hooded her eyes have become, I refrain.

I clear my throat. "There. All gone."

"Thanks."

"No problem."

My phone vibrates on the table. It's a text from a classmate. He's telling me to look to my right. I do so and find him waving me over.

"Who's that?"

"A fellow premed student. I think he needs my help with something. I'll be right back."

I could have asked him via text what he wants, but I need to put distance between Vanessa and me. The atmosphere was getting charged with sexual tension, and I was a moment away from sitting next to her and finishing what we started at her house.

This isn't how I planned for my first months of freedom to go. I wanted to be myself, figure things out on my own.

Now all I want is to make up for lost time with the girl I never forgot.

VANESSA

A GALE of relief whooshes out of me as soon as Paris walks away to talk to his friend. I knew sharing a desk with him was a mistake when my intention in coming to the library was to have a distraction-free study session. If I'd known he'd be here, I'd have steered clear.

I watch him from afar, unable to resist getting my fill. There's a sudden ache in my chest, and I try in vain to massage it away with my fist.

This is not good, Vanessa. You can't jump off the edge when it comes to Paris.

I can't stay here. When he disappears down an aisle with his friend, it's my chance to leave without having to explain why I'm bailing, or worse, him insisting on giving me a lift. Because of my sprained ankle, I can't drive, and Heather is busy with cheer practice. The plan was to get in a couple of hours of solid study and grab an Uber.

I shove my belongings into my backpack as fast as I can and pray that he won't return before I can trudge my way out of the building. Speed walking with crutches is a challenge, but I manage to escape unseen. I move away from the library as fast as I can, just in case Paris decides to look for me before I request a car.

The loud boom of thunder is the only warning I get before the sky falls on me like a waterfall. I search for cover, but the closest awning is the damn library building. I keep moving toward the nearest street corner instead as the cold droplets of rain quickly drench my clothes. My phone is getting wet too, so I try my best to shield it, but the crutches get in the way, and the damn thing slips through my wet fingers.

"Fucking hell."

I drop them so I can bend down and rescue the device before it's ruined. I'm completely soaked now, and what's worse, the app says there aren't any cars available.

"Vanessa!" Paris's loud voice travels through the roar of the storm.

Shit.

I turn around and watch the maniac run after me in the downpour. "What?"

"You left."

"Yeah, I decided to go home."

When he stops mere inches from invading my personal space, I can see that he's not amused.

"Is my company so unbearable that you had to run away in the rain?"

"I wasn't run—"

"Bullshit. You were."

Car headlights illuminate his face, highlighting all his sharp angles and the hard set of his jaw. Man, he's *pissed*.

"If you're so certain, then why did you come after me? That's stalker behavior."

"Stalker..." He rubs his face. "I came after you because I was worried. It's late, raining cats and dogs, and I know you can't drive with a sprained ankle. If that makes me a stalker, then fuck, I guess I am."

Guilt makes me wince. I'm acting like a total bitch because I'm terrified of my feelings and how they're impairing my judgment.

"I was about to order an Uber," I reply meekly.

"No." His voice is hard, leaving no room for argument.

Remorse gives way to irritation. "What do you mean, *no*?"

"I'm taking you home. If after that you want to delete my phone number, block me, and never speak to me again, then fine."

That would remove all the temptation and solve my problem, but it isn't what I want. I should just accept his offer, but that's not what comes out of my mouth.

"You're not the boss of me."

Why am I even fighting him? There aren't any rides available anyway. But his attitude is making me so damn angry. I don't like being told what to do, even if the one doing the telling is the guy I can't stop thinking about.

"You're lucky I'm not your boss." He grabs my crutches from the ground with one hand and then takes my arm with the other. "Come on. I have to get my stuff from the library first."

I plant my feet, refusing to budge. "I'll wait here."

"Yeah, nice try, honey."

"I'm not your *honey*, jackass."

I jerk my arm back, not really expecting to break free of his hold. But we're wet, and he wasn't gripping me too tight. I lose my balance with the momentum, and on reflex, put all my weight on my right foot, which is a monumental mistake. Not only does it not stop my fall, it also hurts like a mother. A yelp escapes my lips.

My back doesn't meet the ground though. Paris catches me, wrapping my body in his arms and pulling me against him. My pulse skyrockets, and any coherent thought flies out of my head. I'm wide eyed when I look up and meet his stare. We don't speak as we drink each other in. Then comes the certainty that if we don't break apart, I might attack his mouth.

"Why are you so difficult?" he whispers, inching closer.

"I'm not." I drop my gaze to his lips for a second, and then go back to his eyes.

"Don't look at me like that," he grumbles.

"Like what?"

He cups my cheek, making me shiver. "Like you want me to kiss you."

"What if I do?"

"Well, then."

His hand finds the back of my head as his lips claim mine. Clutching his biceps, I surrender to his sweet invasion, regretting I didn't succumb to him sooner. The first swipe of his tongue against mine destroys the dam that was keeping all my feelings trapped. They burst through in a violent and devastating flood. I was a fool for believing I could ever move on from him.

He curls his fingers around a strand of my hair and tilts my head to the side as he deepens the kiss. It was fireworks kissing him the first time. Now, it's a comet zooming across the sky, and I can't get enough. If I couldn't forget him then, there's absolutely no chance I'll be able to now.

"Get a room!" someone yells in the distance.

We both ease back, but his arm is still around me, and his hand is in my hair. He rests his forehead against mine, and says, "You have no idea how long I've waited to kiss you again."

"If you say nine years, I'm gonna kick you in the shin," I joke.

He pulls back. "Okay, I won't say nine years then."

I narrow my eyes to slits. "Is that how long?"

Now he really puts distance between us by releasing me. "I kinda don't want to answer now."

I'm back to being mad at him. He gave me the cold shoulder after Cory died, ignored me completely, never even mentioned the heartfelt poem and note I left in his mailbox when I couldn't see him, and in high school, continued his streak of being a total jerk. And now he's claiming he's been into me since then? He was my first crush and first heartbreak.

I cross my arms. "You just did. Let's go get your stuff."

"Okay." He retrieves my discarded crutches and hands them over. "Are you angry with me?"

"No," I reply and then head toward the library.

He matches my pace and walks by my side, but he doesn't utter another word. There's a palpable tension between us now, and I hate it. I wish I could forget how much he hurt me in the past. I understood his silence immediately after his brother's death. He was grieving. And I could ascribe his later cruelty to being young and immature, but then he continued to be a complete tool toward me for most of college.

I know lowering my defenses around him will come back to bite me in the ass. And yet, my lips still tingle from his kiss, and I still yearn for more.

15

PARIS

THE LOOKS I get as I stride back into the library, dripping water, would have been comical if I were in a mood to appreciate them. I can't wrap my mind around what Vanessa wants. She was as into that kiss as I was, but then, bam, an innocent comment has her pulling a one-eighty on me.

She said she'd wait in the lobby, but I wonder if she plans to ditch me again. If she does, I should just let her go, but I can't in good conscience allow her to wander alone at night when it's pouring and she can't defend herself properly.

The visual of her son-of-a-bitch ex assaulting her has been burned into my memory. He's lucky he hasn't crossed my path.

I'm surprised when I find her in the same spot. She's shivering, so I don't think twice before pulling a hoodie from my backpack and offering it to her.

"Here. You can wear this."

She eyes the bunched-up piece of clothing but doesn't take

it. "It's gonna get soaked as well. I'll put it on when I'm in your truck."

"Right." I stuff the hoodie back in my bag. "Wait here. I'll get the truck."

"Leave your backpack with me then. It will get totally wet otherwise."

Man, what's wrong with me? It's like being in her presence has taken away my ability to think. "Good call."

I sprint toward the parking lot. The rain doesn't look like it's going to ease up anytime soon. I don't mind the cold or the wetness, but driving wearing drenched clothes will be hell. I jump in the back seat first and find my gym bag. Unfortunately, the clothes aren't clean. I normally wouldn't give a damn, but I don't want to smell like a rotten egg with Vanessa in my truck. I end up taking the towel and covering the driver's seat instead.

Vanessa walks out of the building the moment I pull up, moving fucking fast for someone on crutches. I get out to help her with those, and that's the only thing she allows me to do. She manages to get into my truck without any help. Better this way. I shouldn't touch her or get near her when she keeps giving me mixed signals.

When I return to my side of the truck and open the door, I find her in her bra. I freeze. "What are you doing?"

"Changing out of my wet shirt. You said I could borrow your hoodie."

I clench my teeth and slide behind the steering wheel, then shut the door hard. What the hell is she trying to do to me? Drive me insane? Fine. Two can play at this game. I remove my wet shirt and toss it to the back of the truck before putting my seat belt on.

"Really, Paris? You're going to drive like that?"

"I don't have a spare, and you're wearing my only dry piece of clothing."

She falls silent, so I dare a peek. It's a big mistake. She looks perfect wearing my clothes, sexy as hell, with her long, tousled damp hair and a pout that only makes me want to kiss her again. I force my gaze back on the road.

"Are you going to tell me why you got angry with me back there?" I ask, because I'm obviously a glutton for punishment.

"If you don't know, I'm not going to tell you," she grumbles.

"That's just fucking dumb. In case you don't already know, men are dense. You have to spell things out for us."

I expect her to pile on to what I just said, but instead, she asks, "Do you remember what happened after our parents caught us kissing?"

"Yeah. They yelled for an eternity and became mortal enemies," I joke, even though that's pretty much what happened.

"No, after that. You stopped talking to me."

I grip the steering wheel tighter. "I was waiting for the dust to settle."

She snorts. "The dust didn't take nine fucking years to settle, Paris."

"I didn't wait *that* long. A week."

"What are you talking about?"

A traffic light turns red, which is providential, because I need to look at her when I say this. "I came looking for you at your soccer practice. I thought I was being sneaky, but your mother saw me and told me that if I didn't leave you alone, she'd send you to live with your grandparents in Brazil."

"What? That's ridiculous. She'd never do that."

"Well, she sounded pretty believable. I didn't want you to get punished because of me, so I decided to wait longer and then..." I look away.

"And then Cory."

"Yeah." My voice is thick, and the knot in my chest tightens.

She doesn't speak for a moment, and I find that I can't say anything else either. The light turns green, and as usual, I wait a couple of seconds before driving. I don't accelerate, and that saves me from colliding with the asshole who runs a red light. He speeds in front of my truck, missing it by a hair. I stomp on the brake hard, and my body lurches forward. The seat belt digs into my bare chest, burning—that's why one shouldn't drive without a shirt on.

"Motherfucker! He could have hit us," Vanessa blurts out.

"Yeah." I slip my hand under the seat belt and rub the chaffed spot.

"Are you okay?"

"I'm fine," I say, sounding harsher than I intended.

Speaking about my brother put me in a funk, and now I just want to get Vanessa home and be alone for a while.

A heavy silence drops over us like a thick blanket, smothering and unyielding. I could turn on the radio but I'm not in the mood to be entertained. I shouldn't let the darkness drag me under again, but I can't find an ounce of motivation to stop it.

When I park in front of Vanessa's house, I say without looking at her, "We're here. You can return my hoodie later."

She exits without a word. I keep my gaze glued to the windshield even when she opens the back door to grab her crutches. A second later, my face gets hit by a ball of fabric.

"Here's your hoodie now. Thanks for the ride." She slams the door shut and trudges to the front door without a shirt on.

Son of a bitch.

I get out of the truck and sprint to catch up with her. "Vanessa, wait."

"Just leave, Paris." She leans one of her crutches against the wall and shoves her now free hand inside her huge bag.

"I planned to, but I can't go without clearing the air between us."

She whips her face to mine while her hand remains buried deep in her bag. "There's nothing to clear. You believed some bullshit lie my mother told you, and then life happened. You picked Lydia, and then decided to match her horrid personality."

The neighbor's front door opens, and on instinct, I step in front of Vanessa, bracing my right arm against the wall behind her, and hiding her from view.

"What are you doing?" she grits out.

"You're half-naked."

"So?"

The neighbor doesn't acknowledge us as he proceeds to take his dog for a night walk. Yet, I don't move, and she doesn't either. One moment we're locked in a battle of stares, the next, I'm claiming her mouth, and pressing my body against hers. Her back meets the front door and she drops the crutches. The air is chilly, but I'm on fire, burning from the inside out for her.

Her fingers thread through my hair, yanking at the strands. "Paris," she murmurs.

I ease back. "Do you want me to leave?"

Her hooded eyes stay locked on my lips. "No, I want to find the damn key in my bag."

I step back, giving her room to rummage through the accessory that seems meant to hide things. She finally fishes out the key with an air of triumph. I don't follow her inside immediately, needing to know she really wants me there.

She looks over her shoulder, and asks, "Are you coming?"

I almost leap inside, pulling her into my arms while I push the door closed with my foot. My mouth finds hers again and, like magic, the darkness that consumed me during the trip here vanishes into thin air. All I needed was my girl.

16

VANESSA

IT's futile to hold on to my grudge, to fight the hurricane of feelings that I kept bottled inside for so long. Paris was an idiot for believing my mother, but he was only thirteen. Then he lost his brother, and that viper Lydia swooped in when I couldn't, thanks to fate fucking up my life.

Or maybe we needed the gap. How many love stories start at the cusp of teenagehood and last more than a few months?

I don't want to think about the past. The moment is now. I'm with Paris, and he's kissing me like he wants to drown in me. I want to touch him everywhere, explore the hard planes of his body, feel the smoothness of his soft skin against my fingertips.

But Heather could come home at any moment, and I don't want her to interrupt us again. Pulling back just a little, I say, "Let's go to my room and get you out of those wet jeans."

Paris's heavy-lidded gaze bounces between my eyes, searching. "Are you sure?"

"Yes. More than anything in the world."

He kisses me hard as he lifts me off the floor. My legs immediately wrap around his hips. Our mouths are fused together when he strides down the hallway.

I pull back suddenly, even though I don't want to interrupt the toe-curling kiss. "Wait. Do you know where we're going?"

"I was waiting for you to tell me." He rubs the space between my eyebrows. "Get rid of this frown, beautiful. I never went exploring at that party last year, save for using the restroom."

"How did you know what I was thinking?"

He kisses the corner of my mouth, and then whispers in my ear. "Because I know you too well."

Desire travels down my back and curls at the base of my spine while goose bumps prickle over my arms. "It's the door to your left."

Without missing a beat, Paris holds me with one arm so he can open the door. He doesn't move farther into the room after he shuts us inside though.

"What is it?" I ask.

He turns half away and glances at the knob. "Your door doesn't lock?"

"Sadly, no. Don't worry. Heather never comes into my room."

His lips split into a devilish grin. "Good. I don't want to hold back for fear of getting caught."

I reciprocate the smile. "Put me down? I want to get rid of these jeans."

"As you wish." He lowers me gently and then drops to his knees in front of me. "Let me help you."

My breath catches when he unzips them and runs his tongue dangerously close to where I desperately want his mouth to be. I thread my fingers through his hair and watch as he pulls the damp fabric down my hips and rolls the jeans off me. Even though it's tricky getting rid of wet pants, he does so easily, and this moment is so hot, I might combust on the spot just watching him.

"God, you're beautiful," he says, right before he kisses my sex through my panties.

Anticipation and lust are making me shake from head to toe, something Paris notices. "I can stop if you want."

"No," I croak. "Please don't."

He skims his hands up and down the sides of my legs. "Are you nervous, kitten?"

A shaky laugh bubbles up my throat, giving me away. "No."

He narrows his heated gaze. "There's no reason to be. Remember, it's me."

I blink fast as I process his words. Doesn't he know I'm a jumble of nerves for that very reason? Or maybe he thinks my reaction is connected to my assault. If anything, I need Paris to erase every memory I have of Ryan.

"I know it's you. I trust you." I cup his cheek.

He turns his face and kisses my palm before looking up again. "I'll make you feel good, gorgeous."

"You already are."

His smile lights up the room and makes my heart soar. This is the point of no return for me. I'm jumping off the edge and I don't care if there's solid ground below or not. I've broken the dam, now I can't pretend anymore I'm not in love with him, always have been.

He pushes my panties aside and licks my clit with a sensuous stroke of his expert tongue, making me see stars. I hold on to his shoulders because I'm turning to putty in his hands.

With a groan, he grips my hips harder, digging his fingers into my skin. His tongue is merciless and is quickly turning me into stardust. I buckle forward when the first wave of orgasm hits me, glad that he has a firm hold on me. He pulls back when

I'm still in the throes of it, but before I can complain, he replaces his mouth with his hand. His thumb flicks my clit left and right while he penetrates me with two fingers.

"That's it, kitten. Come for me."

Nothing comes out of my mouth save for incoherent sounds. I'm breathless and boneless when the wave recedes.

I don't realize I have turned my hands into claws until I see the marks my long nails leave on his shoulder. "I'm so sorry."

Chuckling, he unfurls from his crouch. "Don't be. I didn't feel a thing."

Keeping my eyes glued to his, I rub his erection through his jeans. "We have to remedy that."

He groans, then captures my face between his hands and kisses me while I tease him through his clothes. It's not enough though.

I pull back and whisper against his lips, "Watch me."

It's my turn to kneel before him, a veritable Greek god, and help his cock out of its briefs. I drop my jaw when I see his size. Paris is big *everywhere*. Before he takes my hesitation the wrong way, I wrap my fingers around the base, and lick its length from bottom to top.

"Oh my god, Vanessa." His fingers snake through my hair.

Loving how he says my name like he's dying a little, I bring the soft tip into my mouth and spend a moment playing with the sensitive skin. His grip on my hair increases. He has a thick strand twisted in his fist, and the little bit of pain spurs me on. I swallow his entire length until it hits the back of my throat. I've never deep-throated anyone before, but I'll do anything to drive Paris wild.

"Oh yeah, babe. Just like that." He begins to move his hips, an early attempt to fuck my mouth.

I want him to do it, but not yet. I'm having too much fun exploring, learning what he likes. I pull back just enough to keep my lips around the head while I work him with my hand.

My fingers glide up and down easily, and he seems to grow larger with each stroke.

"I want all the way in your filthy mouth again, kitten," he says in a voice that's tight with need.

I suck him again, loving his taste, the feel of his cock against my tongue.

"That's it, babe. Suck me harder."

He thrusts his hips forward, and this time, I do let him take control. His grunts of pleasure and his dirty mouth are making my clit throb again. I might come just from listening to him.

He's rough and demanding, but I can take it. I can take all of him. He's pulling my hair harder now, and I don't think he realizes it yet, but it feels so damn good.

"Fuck! I'm gonna come."

He tries to pull out, but I grab his butt cheeks and keep him where he is. His cock throbs against my tongue as his release fills my mouth. I drink it all, and when it's all gone, I'm sad there isn't more. He goes perfectly still for a moment, and the grip he has on my hair lessens. I ease back, releasing him with a wet pop, and let my knees fold until I'm sitting on the balls of my feet.

His expression is soft as he looks at me, but it changes in a flash to something close to remorse. He drops into a crouch in front of me and asks, "Did I hurt you, babe?"

"Uh, what? No."

He watches me closely. "Are you sure?"

I nod. "Yeah. I never knew you had such a dirty mouth."

His lips twitch as if he can't decide if he should smile or continue to worry. "I never talked like that before, but with you..." He picks up a lock of my hair and lets it run through his fingers. "You drive me crazy, kitten."

Pure elation spreads through my chest. I'm insanely happy that his ex never got to see this side of him.

"I want more of you, Paris." I get back on my feet, pulling him with me.

He quirks an eyebrow. "How much more?"

Making sure I don't put any weight on my right foot, I rise on my tiptoes and kiss his jaw. "Everything."

He slants his lips over mine, kissing me hard and fast before stepping back. He yanks his jeans and underwear all the way down and then steps out of them. He makes a motion in my direction, but I raise my hand, halting him.

"Hold on for just a second. Let me take a moment to appreciate the view."

He gives me a crooked smile. "Fine, but only if you get rid of that." He points at my bra.

"I suppose that's fair." I reach behind my back and release the clasp.

I don't break eye contact as I lower each strap individually and finally let the bra fall at my feet.

Paris's Adam's apple bobs up and down as he swallows hard. "Damn it. You're breathtaking."

I drop my gaze to his ripped chest and abs and try to make out all the ink he has there. "So are you. When did you start getting those?"

"Two years after Cory died." He touches a spot on his left pec. "I got this one for him."

I look closer so I can read the quote. My heart lurches in my chest when I recognize the words. It's a quote from the poem I wrote him. *In the darkness, I shall remember how your gaze brightened everything.*

"I... I didn't think you cared about that."

He frowns. "Do you know where this is from?"

His question takes me aback. "Of course I do. I wrote it."

He stares at me without blinking, without breathing. "*You* wrote it?" He gets the words out as if he's having a hard time processing them.

"Yes. I wrote you a letter, and the poem. I stuck the envelope in your mailbox the day after Cory died."

Paris's face becomes paler. He shuffles back until he sits on the edge of my mattress, holding his head in his hands. "I can't believe this."

"Can't believe what?"

He looks up. "Lydia gave me that poem. She said she wrote it."

My stomach clenches painfully. And then comes the rage. "That lying *bitch*. She must have stolen the letter and copied the poem."

His blue eyes become glassy as he holds my stare. "I had no idea. This poem meant so much to me. Now I feel a million times worse for all the things I did to you. Especially that ridiculous stunt at prom."

I'm angry as fuck that Lydia lied to him, that she drove us apart, but I also hate hearing the sadness in his voice. I close the distance between us and capture his face between my hands. "I don't want to think about the past, or all the moments that snake stole from us. I just want to be with you."

He reaches for my face and rubs my cheek. "Same, kitten."

Our mouths meet as we drop onto the mattress. The kiss is unhurried at first, but the fire between us can't be contained. I fall on my back with Paris on top of me. His cock presses against my belly, already rock hard.

I open my legs wide for him, lifting my knees. He releases my lips to continue his torture down my neck and then my chest. His large hand covers one of my breasts while his tongue teases my other nipple to the point that I'm begging for another release. I've had fun in the bedroom before, but never in my life has a guy turned me on so much that I could orgasm without penetration or clit stimulation. I didn't even think it was possible until now.

"Paris, I need more."

He lifts his sexed-up face to look at me. "Me too, gorgeous. Where do you keep your condoms?"

"Nightstand."

He doesn't even need to move to reach the drawer. He pulls the box out and flips it over. Only one packet falls from it. We both don't speak for a long stretch. Is he thinking about how often Ryan and I had sex?

"Well..." He picks up the condom. "I guess we have to make this last a really long time."

"Fine by me. There's no limit to how many times I can climax during one fuck."

He watches me through narrowed eyes as he rips the packet open. "It's okay, kitten. I have good stamina."

My gaze inevitably drops to his erection, and a sliver of nervousness returns to my chest. We're really doing this. I never allowed myself to fantasize about sleeping with Paris, because I never thought it would happen. I sincerely believed I had lost him to that leech forever. Now I'm terrified I'm going to suck.

He rolls the condom down his length and returns to his position between my legs. But before he lowers his body to mine completely, he rests his forearms on each side of my shoulders and really looks at me.

"What?" I ask.

"I'm giving you the chance to change your mind."

"Paris..."

"I don't want to mess things up between us anymore. I'm done hurting you without realizing it."

My heart skips a beat. Here he is being one-hundred-percent Paris, something I thought I hated, and yet the butterflies in my stomach say otherwise. "The only way you can screw things up is if you don't shut up and fuck me already."

His eyes widen a fraction, and then he leans back and lifts one of my legs, setting it over his shoulder. His fingers wrap around his shaft, then he pumps it a couple of times, not breaking eye contact. The visual makes me hornier, so much so, that I bring my fingers to my pussy and play with myself too.

A groan comes from deep in his throat. He places his cock right at my entrance, and says, "If getting railed by me is what you want, kitten...."

In one powerful move, he sheathes himself in me, making me cry out. He's filling me completely, stretching me to the max. This isn't my first time, but it feels like it could be. He rotates his hips without pulling back, letting me get used to his girth.

"How does it feel, babe?"

"Do you really want to know?" I peer at him through half-open eyes.

He reaches over and rubs his thumb over my lower lip. "Yes."

"I'm not sure. Move your hips again." I give him a wicked grin.

Instead of gyrating his pelvis like before, he pulls back halfway and then slowly fills me once more. "Like that?"

I close my eyes and hum. "Yeah, like that. It feels good, really good."

He slides his hand down my chest and grabs one of my breasts, kneading it as he proceeds to fuck me properly. Man, this is even better. I can't concentrate anymore.

"Now it's your turn," I breathe out. "Confess."

"I love fucking your tight pussy, babe," he grunts. "Never had anything better."

A shadow of doubt crosses my mind. Is he telling me the truth, or is that just dirty talk?

"I can tell by your face that you don't believe me." He leans forward, keeping my leg firmly resting over his shoulder. I'm lucky that I'm flexible, because he's stretching me in more ways than one like this. "I'm not lying, kitten. I swear to God." He kisses me slowly, matching the tempo of his thrusts. I throw my arms around his neck, needing him closer as I melt into the mattress.

There's a sudden shift between us. The pace increases, our tongues dancing together with more fury, more passion. The headboard bangs loudly against the wall, mixing with the creaking of the bed. We might end up breaking it, but I don't care. The world could end, and I wouldn't make him stop.

It's fortunate our mouths are fused together when I climax, because it's violent and earth shattering, and I'd have screamed at the top of my lungs otherwise.

"I'm sorry, babe," he says a moment later against my lips.

"Why are you apologizing?"

"Because I'm... motherfucker," he groans, and pounds into me faster and faster. His cock thickens, grows harder, and pulses inside of me.

He slows down and rests his forehead against mine. His breathing is coming out in bursts when he says, "I couldn't hold on any longer. That's why I was apologizing."

His confession makes me laugh. "Dude, you gave me the best orgasms of my life."

He leans back and studies me. "Did I? For real?"

I nod. "Now get off me before you make the condom pointless."

He kisses my nose first. "You're cute when you're bossy."

My leg hurts a little from being in that awkward position for so long, but I try to hide that from Paris. He slides off me and gets out of bed. It's only then that I think of a reply.

Leaning on my elbows, I say, "So that means I'm always cute."

He looks over his shoulder, and smiles. "You're gorgeous."

A blush creeps up my cheeks. Luckily, Paris heads into the bathroom to dispose of the condom, and I don't have to hide my reaction from him. I collapse on the bed and stare at the ceiling while sporting a grin that I'm sure is the goofiest ever.

Paris returns a moment later, and I have to force the smile from my face. I get off the bed and veer to the bathroom to freshen up, kind of dreading the post-sex talk. But when I return to the room, he's out.

I guess we don't need to talk tonight. I slide in next to him and fall asleep so fast, I don't have time to worry about tomorrow.

17

VANESSA

I WAKE up with someone kissing my shoulder. At first, I think I'm dreaming, but then the last vestiges of sleep ebb away. The solid chest pressed against my back reminds me this isn't a dream. I slept with Paris, and he ended up spending the night. I wait for apprehension to hit me. He's my first love and heartbreak, and I've been wrestling with my feelings—lust, longing, and fear—for a while. But the anxiety doesn't come, maybe because, not satisfied with kissing me, he runs his fingers down my stomach.

Letting out a sigh, I snuggle closer. "Hmm, I could get used to waking up like this."

"Me too." He bites my shoulder gently as his fingers glide between my legs, finding my folds already slick with desire.

He slides down the bed and turns me on my back at the same time. The sheet is partially covering us, and before he disappears underneath it, he locks his heated gaze with mine, making it difficult to breathe.

"Have I told you how glorious you look in the morning?" he asks and places an open-mouth kiss below my belly button.

I shiver. "No, and it'd be a lie anyway."

"Not from where I am. Now let's find out if you taste as sweet as last night."

He moves farther south, disappearing from view. Instead of peppering a trail of kisses down my belly, he slides his warm tongue all the way to my center and, when he gets to my clit, he licks my bundle of nerves nice and slow.

I twist my fingers around the sheet beneath me, arching my back as a desperate moan escapes my lips. "Oh, Paris. *Yes.*"

He alternates between licking and sucking my clit into his mouth. My toes are already curling, and he's only just begun. This proves that last night's performance wasn't a fluke. He's not only a feast for the eyes, he's also a god in bed. In less than a minute, he has me panting. He nudges my legs farther apart, and then flattens his palm on my pubic bone and eats my pussy as if it's the best thing he's ever had. I can already feel the telltale signs that an orgasm isn't far. My nipples are as hard as little pebbles. Closing my eyes, I play with them, heightening my pleasure.

The hinges of my bedroom door creak loudly a second before Heather says, "Hey, have you... oh my god."

My eyes fly open, and I'd have jumped into a sitting position if Paris wasn't between my legs. "Heather! What the hell!"

"Sorry! I didn't know you made up with Ryan." She begins to back away, but then Paris's head pops from under the sheet.

"She did *not* make up with that asshole," he growls.

If I wasn't dying of mortification, I'd take pleasure in Heather's reaction. Her eyes bug out of her skull cartoon style. Then she squints. "I *knew* there was something going on between you two."

"Get out!" I toss my pillow at her.

She finally does, shutting the door. I close my eyes and pinch my nose. "Kill me now."

"And you said she would never barge in here." He laughs.

I open my eyes and glare. "This has *never* happened before. Maybe she knew you were here and wanted to catch us."

Paris folds his arms over my tummy and rests his chin on top of them. "My truck *is* parked right out front."

"Ugh! One more reason to kill her."

"Do you want to do that after I get you off?" He wiggles his eyebrows up and down.

I don't know if I should laugh or yell. "No. She killed the mood." I push him off me and get up.

"Yeah, I should get going anyway. I don't want to be a witness to murder. That could hinder my chances of getting into a good med school."

"You're making fun of me, and I don't appreciate it." I grab a pair of clean undies from the chest of drawers and put them on hastily.

Paris finds his jeans and wrinkles his nose. "Damn. I should have hung these in the bathroom to dry."

Remorse dampens my anger a little. "Crap. I totally forgot about it too. Are they still super wet?"

"Damp, but hell, nothing for it now."

He gets dressed and I simply watch. Never mind that I'm still wearing only a pair of panties.

He notices, and with a sexy smile, walks over. "I think that maybe you *do* want me to finish what I started." He circles my waist with his strong arms.

"The issue is that I'll want more, and we're out of condoms."

He twists his face into an exaggerated frown. "True. I'll stop by the drugstore later. We won't want for condoms, kitten."

And here comes the dreaded morning-after talk.

"About that... what exactly are we doing?"

He grows serious and it's not an act now. "Honestly, I wasn't planning on jumping into another serious relationship."

Disappointment floods through me. I should be on the same page—I just got out of a relationship. But it's Paris, and I'm in love with him.

"Yeah, same." I try to pull away, but he holds me against him.

"You didn't let me finish. It wasn't the plan, because I never thought you'd give me the time of day."

"Oh."

He traces my hairline with the tips of his fingers. "I won't lose you again, babe."

My heart overflows with emotion, and if I'm not careful, I might blurt out the truth and surely scare the crap out of him. Who says the *L* word after one hookup? Crazy people. I don't want him to think I'm from the same psycho town as Lydia.

"What are you saying, Paris? Do you want to date me?"

"I do." He kisses my neck, making my eyes flutter. "But I think we should keep things on the down-low for now."

I pull back and look him in the eye. "Why?"

Letting out a sigh, he steps back, releasing me. I miss the contact immediately. "Well, there's the issue of our families. I want to date you without the drama."

I cross my arms. "We can't avoid our parents forever. But it's more than that, isn't it?"

He pinches his lips together, and his eyes look hella guilty now. "Yeah, there's the Lydia factor. We are one-hundred-percent over, at least on my part, but you saw her on the quad. She's clearly not ready to let me go. And after what you told me about the stolen poem...."

"What? You don't believe she did that?"

"That's not what I'm saying at all. I believe you. But knowing what she did... it just proves that she isn't a stable person."

"That's too fucking bad. Paris, you can't make life decisions around her moods."

His expression is pained, which makes me want to scream.

"I know. I'm trying to spare you."

"I don't need your protection. I can handle any shade she throws my way. Don't use her as an excuse to keep this quiet because you're afraid to hurt Lydia's precious feelings."

"I don't care about her feelings." Rubbing his jaw, he glances away. "I think I've already fucked this up. I should go."

My stomach drops through the earth. That's it? He's just going to walk away because I don't agree with his idiotic thought process?

"Yeah, I guess you should."

"I'll call you later."

I almost say *don't bother*, but that would be childish. I end up not saying a word, but I don't miss the fact that he walks out of my room without kissing me goodbye.

I turn away from the door as tears gather in my eyes. I *knew* this was too good to be true. I trusted Paris, and he once again smashed my heart to pieces.

Ugh. I'm so fucking stupid. Maybe I shouldn't have lost my temper so quickly and tried to see it from his side.

The door opens again, and I'm ready to tell Heather to get lost, but arms hug me from behind, and Paris's mouth kisses my shoulder.

"I'm sorry, kitten. I'm an idiot."

The anger swirling in my chest is quickly replaced by relief. He came back, and I can't help melting into his body. "Yes, you are."

"You're right. I can't keep my happiness on hold because other people are miserable, or in her case, insane." He turns me around in his arms. "I want to be with you."

I search his eyes and find nothing but honesty in them. It makes me feel guilty that I was quick to judge his motivation. If

I'd been in his shoes and found out my ex had been lying to me for years, I'd go nuclear on his ass. But Paris isn't like me. Raging jealousy made me react that way. I don't want Lydia taking up any more space in his mind than she already did. I have to trust him, or this will never work.

"I want to be with you too. And maybe it wouldn't be the end of the world if we don't broadcast that we're together yet. I'm not saying that to spare Lydia—I actually want her to rot in hell. But it'd be nice to get to know you without the world intruding."

"Are you saying you want to date me in secret?"

I shrug. "Why not? It could be fun sneaking around. And major bonus points for avoiding parental drama."

"Yeah, but can Heather keep a secret?" He arches an eyebrow.

"Oh, I've been saving up dirt on her for a long time. She'll keep mine if I keep hers."

"Now I'm curious."

"If I tell you, then I'll lose my bargaining chip."

He cradles my face between his hands and claims my lips. This should be a see-you-later kiss, not the fire-starter kind. I'm regretting not letting him finish his tongue play after Heather barged in.

As if reading my mind, he says, "Sit on my face, kitten."

"What about you?"

He bites my earlobe softly, then whispers in my ear, "Oh, don't worry, I'm gonna enjoy myself thoroughly."

18

PARIS

I'VE BEEN WALKING around campus with the biggest smile, so it's no surprise that when I meet up with Danny and Puck at Zuko's Diner to grab a quick lunch, I can't wipe it off my face. Perhaps I should tone it down. It's not my MO to be this chipper, but hell, I don't want to. Not even the knowledge of Lydia's lies is going to bring me down. I'll deal with her later.

"What's up, boys?" I ask as I slide into Puck's side of the booth seat. "Did you order already?"

"Nah, we just got here," Puck replies. "We were waiting for you and Rossi."

"Oh, I didn't know Andy was coming." I reach for the menu.

"Yeah, apparently Puck has news he'd like to share with all of us in person." Danny gives Puck a meaningful glance.

"I hope he's not late as usual. I'm starving. I could eat everything they have here," I say.

Someone whacks me upside the head with a menu. "I'm not always late, jackass."

Andreas sits across from me and pushes his aviator sunglasses onto his head. I rub the spot where he hit me, but not even his antics are going to sour my mood.

I notice his leather jacket, and say, "Tom Cruise called and wants his *Top Gun* outfit back."

"Well, he can sit and wait." Andreas smirks, not falling for my bait. I chuckle nonetheless, making him frown. "Wait. Did I just hear Paris laugh? Did I miss something?"

"If you did, we all did. I have no idea what's gotten into him," Puck replies.

"He probably got laid," Danny chimes in.

The menu becomes very interesting all of a sudden. I keep my gaze down, pretending to scan the offerings when I already know what I want.

"Holy shit! He totally did." Andreas smacks his hand on the table, rattling the condiments tray. "All right. Spill. We want a name."

"I'm not going to kiss and tell."

"That's right, Paris. Those things should remain private," Puck pipes up.

As the most religious dude in our group, it makes sense that he believes that. I grew up in a churchgoing family too, but my folks are only superzealous when it suits their interests. As for me, I just follow along to avoid headaches.

"Of course you believe that." Andreas shakes his head and glances at the menu. "How's that chastity vow working out for you?"

"It's going great. Now can we stop focusing on Andino's love life for a second so I can tell you why I wanted you here?"

"Hooray to that," I say.

"You have our undivided attention, Puck," Danny replies.

"Hold on. I got to make a call first." He pulls out his phone and presses the video chat button. A moment later, Troy's face appears on the scream. The former quarterback for the Rebels, he's been living in London with his girlfriend since he graduated a year ago, and I haven't seen him since.

"Hey, Puck. What's up, man? Long time."

"I know. The whole gang is here." He turns his camera so Troy can get a visual of all of us.

We all wave at the camera and say hello before Puck sets his phone against the window and Troy has a view of the entire table.

"I'm dying here, man," Troy says. "What's going on that you need all of us together?"

"Duh, can't you guess?" Andreas answers before Puck can. "He's getting married."

I kick him under the table. "Dude. Shut up!"

"Ouch," he complains.

"Never mind Rossi, Paris. He loves to be a dick." Puck laughs. "But anyway, that's exactly why I wanted you all here. Mia and I are getting married next month, and I want you guys to be my groomsmen."

"In a month?" My brows arch. "What's the hurry?"

"Oh my god, Andino. Are you thick? It's a shotgun wedding." Andreas laughs.

Danny scowls. "You don't know that."

Puck rubs the back of his neck. "Actually, that's why. Mia is pregnant."

That only makes Andreas laugh harder. "Chastity vow my ass."

"Wow, congratulations, man." Troy interrupts Andy's antics. "Count me in."

"Yeah, me too. And congrats," I add.

"Same," Danny says, "And you are happy about it, right?"

Considering he grew up without knowing who his father was and then later found out the man was a total douche, I don't find it strange that he's asking.

"I couldn't be happier. I've always known Mia was the one."

"But what happened to the chastity vow? I thought you were dead serious about that," Andreas asks without mirth. I guess he's done making fun of Puck.

"Yes, we were, but after Mia's cousin passed away unexpectedly, we decided that life was unpredictable."

A shadow drops over me. I know too well what the sudden death of a loved one can do. In my case, I jumped into a toxic relationship. Puck's outcome is far better than mine was.

"Since you guys are all there, I might as well tell you my news too," Troy pipes up.

Andreas sits straighter and his brows arch as he says, "Don't fucking tell me you proposed to Charlie without telling me beforehand."

Troy rolls his eyes. "I wouldn't dream of doing that to you."

Danny and I chuckle. Since I'm sitting across from Andreas, I get the full blast of his glare.

"What's the news?" Danny brings the conversation on track.

"We're moving back to California. Charlie and I both got offered jobs in LA."

We all take turns congratulating Troy on his move, and then he says he needs to run errands. We're ready to order when the bell chime draws my attention to the diner's entrance.

Ryan walks in with one of his douchey friends, and my entire body tenses. "That motherfucker," I say under my breath.

"Who are you talking about?" Andreas turns to look, and so does Danny.

"Who's that?" Puck asks.

"A frat-boy asshole," Andreas replies.

My tight grip on the edge of the table is the only thing keeping my ass on the booth seat. Ryan doesn't glance in our direction, and he should thank his lucky stars that he doesn't get assigned a booth on our side of the diner.

"What did he ever do to you?" Danny asks.

I'm seething as I try to control my rage, so I don't answer right away.

"Shit. He must have done something awful. Paris is about to blow," Andreas replies.

My appetite is gone, and I know that if I stay a moment longer, I won't be able to contain myself. I'll march to that fuckwad and do what I should have done the night he attacked Vanessa.

I get up suddenly. "I can't be here."

"Bro, wait up," Andreas says, but I don't listen.

I stride toward the exit, trying my best to not look toward Ryan. My hand is on the knob when I hear his laughter. I turn and see he's at the farthest booth from the front. My body is already moving to head that way when a hand on my shoulder stops me.

"Whatever he did, you're in no condition to confront him now," Andreas tells me.

"Bullshit," I say, even though he's right.

"Bullshit my ass. You have murder in your eyes, Andino. Come on, let's get out of here." He opens the door and practically has to shove me out, because I'm rooted to the floor.

My rage doesn't simmer down once I'm in the parking lot. I'm filled to the max with it. Puck and Danny also followed and are crowding me now. They're blocking me from running back inside.

"Are you going to tell us why seeing Ryan Watergate made you go berserk?" Andreas asks.

"I can't tell you." I begin to pace. "Fuck! I want to kill that asshole."

"Let's get out of here then, before you have the chance," Andreas says.

"I came with Puck, so I'll ride with Paris," Danny says, as if I'm not there.

I turn around to glare at the trio. "I don't need a fucking babysitter."

"No offense, bro, but you do," Puck replies. "Go on, Danny. Take Paris away before he explodes."

Danny presses his hand against my back and nudges me toward my truck. He wouldn't be able to move me if I put up a fight, but the sane part of my brain is slowly regaining control. I get behind the steering wheel and take a couple of deep breaths while I wait for Danny to get in.

"Are you okay to drive?" he asks as soon as he shuts the door.

"Yep." I put the truck in gear and accelerate too fast, burning rubber.

"Jesus, take it easy, man."

I ease off the gas pedal, managing to maintain the speed limit.

Danny lets me stew for a few minutes before he opens his mouth. "You don't need to tell me why you wanted to pummel Ryan, but is it something you can get over, or do I need to worry about it?"

I clutch the steering wheel tighter, clenching my jaw. "I'm not sure I can get over it."

Danny rubs his face and curses. "What can we do then, to avoid you getting in trouble if you decide to punish the bastard?"

"Keep him away from me."

"Yeah, that's not gonna work. We aren't attached to your hip, or his. Maybe if you told me why you hate his guts, then it'd be easier to help you fight the urge to annihilate him."

"I hear what you're saying, but unfortunately, I'd be betraying someone's trust if I told you."

"Can't you tell me what he's done without revealing your friend's name?"

I'm fucking torn. I'm bound to cross paths with Ryan again,

and if today was any indication, I will *end* him. Then what? Get kicked off the team, expulsion, arrest? Maybe telling Danny would help, but even if I don't reveal Vanessa's name, I still feel like I'm betraying her trust.

"This stays between us, all right? No one can know, not even Andy or Sadie."

"Bro, you can trust me."

"I caught Ryan sexually assaulting someone outside of Tailgaters one night. I stopped him, but the victim didn't want to press charges. Which... I get it. But I'm still fucking mad that the motherfucker did that and wasn't punished for it."

"Man, that's fucked up. Now I get why you wanted to go savage on him. I'd probably have the same reaction."

I laugh without humor. "No, you wouldn't. You're the most chill guy I know."

"Not when someone I care about is involved. Sadie was attacked in London before she moved to LA. I can tell you now because she's fine with people knowing."

"No shit. I'm sorry, man."

"Yeah, she got stabbed trying to protect a friend from some drunks. Sometimes when I see her scar, I get a burst of anger. If the guy who did that to her crossed my path, I'd probably destroy him."

"Thanks for telling me, man. I don't know if it will help contain my anger, but I'm glad I'm not the only one who's protective of the ones they love."

"So, this is about Lydia, then?"

Shit. I can't believe I let that fucking comment slip. I can't let Danny believe Lydia was attacked. That wouldn't be right.

"No, Lydia wasn't the victim."

It takes a couple of beats for the coin to drop. "Oh shit. It was the girl who put that smile on your face earlier. I didn't know it was already that serious. I thought it was just a hookup."

"It wasn't just a hookup, and that's all I'm going to say."

"Fair. I'm done prying."

Vanessa's identity is a secret, but for how long? We don't plan to hide that we're dating forever. When we come out, Danny will know she was the girl Ryan attacked. Then my betrayal will be complete.

I'm so fucking consumed by my guilt that it's not until I drop Danny off that it dawns on me... I not only gave him too many clues about Vanessa, but I also confessed that I love her. I knew before last night that my feelings for her were deep, but I didn't think I was already in love with her.

I guess now I know.

19

VANESSA

I SPEND an hour getting ready for my first stay-in date with Paris. Since we want to keep our relationship a secret, not going out in public is a must. So we agreed to takeout and a movie at home. I'm probably overdressed for it. I'm wearing my favorite pair of jeans, the ones that make my ass look fucking amazing, and a pretty top with a low neckline to show off my cleavage. I'd be wearing heels too, if it weren't for my sprained ankle.

I asked Heather if she could spend the night at her boyfriend Leo's place, so when I find her in the kitchen eating instant noodles, my disposition sours.

"What are you still doing here?"

"Relax. I'm leaving as soon as I finish dinner."

"You couldn't eat at Leo's?"

"I'm hungry now."

Glowering, I cross my arms. "You'd better not be here when Paris arrives."

"And if I am, so what? I've already seen everything." She smirks.

"I still think you knew he was in my room when you barged in."

Unfazed, she swallows a mouthful of noodles. "Think whatever you want. I don't get why you want to date him in secret though. You guys have been into each other for a long time. Anyone with a pair of eyes could see that."

"That's such bullshit. Paris and I barely interacted with each other at Rushmore unless he was defending his ex."

"If you say so." She shrugs.

"I do. Anyway, family drama and that fucking bitch drove us apart the first time. We want to date in peace for a while."

"Oh please. You were only thirteen. There's no chance a relationship then would have lasted more than a few months."

She couldn't be more wrong, and the thought makes my stomach coil tightly.

"Right, then explain to me why Paris dated Lydia for so long."

Heather sets down her bowl and grows serious. "Lydia is a conniving snake. She took advantage of Paris's grief to sink her claws into him. And didn't you just find out that she stole your poem and claimed she wrote it?"

I grimace. I told Heather the story this morning. "Don't remind me. I want to punch her in the throat for that one alone."

"But you can't do it because of your position on the Ravens. I get it. Maybe I can get revenge for you." She smiles in a chilling way.

I narrow my eyes. "You've been watching too much Netflix."

"So? Do you want to know why Paris put up with all her bullshit?"

My spine goes taut as my interest piques. It seems Heather

knows more about the details of Paris and Lydia's relationship than I do.

I wave my hand. "Go on. You're going to tell me anyway."

"Every time she wanted to manipulate Paris into doing something, she threatened to kill herself."

My blood turns cold, and a new knot forms in my chest. "How do you know that?"

She shrugs. "I can't remember where I heard the story, but it didn't come from only one source. You can't tell me it doesn't fit her personality to pull shit like that. Can you imagine what that was like for Paris? I mean, he lost his brother to suicide."

I hug my middle, feeling wretched. "He probably felt he couldn't let that happen again."

"Exactly." She rinses her bowl and sticks it in the dishwasher. "Anyway, I'd better go. I don't want to make Paris uncomfortable with my presence."

In a daze, I veer for the couch. It takes a couple minutes for Heather to leave, but I know she does when the front door bangs shut. I'm reeling from what she told me, sad beyond measure that Paris had to deal with that fucker for so long. I really should beat the shit out of her for all the suffering she caused. I don't realize I'm crying until I feel moisture on my cheeks. Damn it. There goes my makeup.

I jump from the couch, ready to run—more like hop—to my bathroom to check the damage, but a knock on the front door stops me short. Shit. It must be Paris. I don't want to make him wait outside. I change direction, but before I open the door for him, I look at my reflection in the mirror and wipe the corners of my eyes. The smudging was minimal.

I open the door with a smile that's a little forced. It changes into something genuinely radiant when I see Paris standing there in all his six-foot-four glory, holding a bouquet of pink roses along with the take-out containers. My heart does a somersault in my chest as tingles of excitement ripple through my body.

"Hi," I say.

"Hello, kitten."

I step back to allow him in, and then close the door. The smell of delicious Chinese food invades the space, but even though I was hungry before, food is now the last thing on my mind.

"Are those for me?" I eye the roses when all he does is stare at me with a grin.

"Ah, yes." He hands over the bouquet. "I was a little distracted."

I bring the flowers to my nose before I thank him for them. "They're beautiful."

"Not as beautiful as you."

I laugh, making Paris blush. He rubs the back of his neck. "Sorry. That was corny."

Stepping into his space, I kiss his cheek. "Lucky for you, I love corny."

His free arm snakes around my waist, pulling me flush against his body. His mouth finds mine next, and I melt into his embrace. If I could, I'd never stop kissing him. Happiness should be the only thing pumping into my heart, but instead, overwhelming sadness breaks through. I could have had him like this for much longer if Lydia hadn't interfered.

Reluctantly, I pull back. "I'd better put these in a vase."

I sense him watching me as I limp to the kitchen. I don't care to use the crutches in the house, so moving around is a little slow.

He follows me and sits on a high stool by the kitchen counter, setting the food there. "Is something wrong?"

I whip my face in his direction. "What? No. Why are you asking?"

His gaze narrows. "Kitten, don't lie to me. You look sad. Did something happen?"

Giving my attention to the flowers, I don't answer him. I don't know what to say without bringing up Lydia, and I really don't want to remind Paris of his ex.

"Vanessa..."

I let out a heavy sigh and look into his eyes again. "I want to tell you something."

He sits straighter in his chair. "Okay."

"I didn't abandon you when you lost your brother. When I found out what happened, I begged my parents to take me to see you. They didn't think it was a good idea, despite my pleas. I went anyway on my bike. But when I got there, Lydia answered the door, and she wouldn't let me through. Then another woman showed up—I think she was your aunt. I mean, she looked a bit like your mother. Anyway, she told me you weren't in any condition to see anyone. I left, and it started to rain heavily." I touch the faint scar near my elbow.

"What happened?"

"I was almost hit by a car, ended up falling off my bike and breaking my arm. That's why I didn't see you. I wound up in the ER, and after that, my parents grounded me. I did convince my father to drive me to your house the next day to deliver the letter. But when my parents finally eased off my punishment, you were..." I drop my gaze to the counter. "It didn't look like you needed me anymore."

"She was just a friend then. She didn't become my girlfriend until freshman year of high school."

"Well, same difference."

He walks around the counter and pulls me into his arms. "I'm glad you told me. I'm also a bit mad that you could have gotten really hurt because of me."

"I was heartbroken for you. I wanted to be there."

He caresses my cheek with the back of his hand. "But is that why you're sad? It's in the past, kitten. All that matters is that we're together now."

I lower my gaze to the hollow of his throat, trying to hide the truth. It's probably pointless. He must see it in my eyes. I don't want to reveal what Heather told me though.

"I was sad because, thanks to my parents being stubborn mules, the accident, and Lydia acting like a soap opera villain, you got stuck in an unhealthy relationship."

He pinches my chin with his forefinger and thumb and lifts my face. "Maybe I had to go through that to appreciate what I have now."

He's right. I'm acting like a Debbie Downer.

I lift my right foot and then rise on the tip of my toes with my left so I can reach Paris's mouth. We don't waste time with small kisses. Our mouths crash together hungrily, impatient, and I know dinner will be forgotten for a while. He picks me up and goes straight to my room. I don't notice the plastic bag in his hand until he sets me down on the bed and empties it over the mattress. Three large boxes of condoms bounce off.

"Oh my god. Did you get a month's supply?"

"One month? Are you insane? That won't last a week." He grabs the hem of his T-shirt and peels it off.

His pecs and arms flex, making my mouth water. I know exactly what I'm doing to him first. I stand up and push him onto the bed.

"What are you doing, kitten?" he asks through a smile.

"I'm taking charge." I flatten my palms against his solid chest and nudge him back. "Lie down and let me have my fun."

His eyes turn smoldering in a flash. He cups the back of my head and pulls me to him for another gloriously hot kiss. Desire pools between my legs, making my clit throb. Maybe I shouldn't have worn jeans.

Before Paris decides to take control, I pull back and push off him so I can get rid of my clothes. He leans up on his elbows and watches me through hooded eyes. I take off my pants first but leave my underwear on. My long top covers them. Paris doesn't seem to mind. His attention is on my thighs, and his heated gaze feels like a caress.

"I love what soccer does for you, babe."

My lips curl into a grin. "I bet you do, but these have nothing to do with sports." I pull my top off and lob it to the side. I'm not wearing a bra, so instantly, Paris's gaze fixes on my breasts.

He stretches out an arm. "Come here, kitten. Let me feast on your lovely tits."

I wag my forefinger. "Oh no, sir. I said I was in charge, and I want to feast on *you*."

I straddle his thighs and then lower my mouth to his chest, licking the area around his nipple. He hisses, and then curls his fingers around a strand of my hair. I tease him a bit before biting softly, then I switch to the other side. While my tongue is busy, I run my fingers up and down his washboard abs, stopping my caress when my fingers reach the waistband of his pants.

"Vanessa, babe, what are you doing to me?" he asks in a raspy whisper.

"I'm exploring."

I pepper open kisses down his stomach, loving how he responds to me. His breathing is shallow, and his erection is straining against the fabric of his jeans.

"I want to explore too."

"Soon."

I unbutton his pants, and then open his fly slowly. Paris, impatient man that he is, lifts his ass and pushes the fabric as low as he can.

"Hey, I was going to do that," I complain halfheartedly.

"I'll let you peel them off my legs—just please get rid of them."

I was planning on tasting him, but I can't say no when he sounds like he's about to die.

I should have known it was a ruse. I need to slide off him to remove his jeans, and no sooner are they gone than he tackles me, flipping me over on the mattress so he's on top.

"Hey, that's not fair. I call foul play."

"Sorry, kitten. You weren't playing fair either." He thrusts his hips forward, rubbing his hard cock against my core.

We're both still wearing our underwear, but the friction alone is making me light-headed. Or maybe it's the skillful way he mingles his tongue with mine, taking and giving in equal measure. I forget my original plan and surrender to him. He's in no hurry to fuck me though. Instead, he mimics what's to come, grinding his pelvis against mine. My panties are soaked through when I climax out of the blue. I usually know when it's about to happen. Not this time.

"Oh my god, Paris. Don't stop," I beg him between feverish kisses.

He grunts in response, making me wonder why he isn't as chatty as the last time. I miss his filthy mouth, but I don't mind what his tongue is doing one bit. My body relaxes against the mattress as the wave of my release subsides.

He pulls back, resting his forearms on the mattress. "How are you feeling, kitten?"

"Pretty good." I smile.

"Do you know what I want to do now?" He runs his fingers over my collarbone.

"Eat dinner?"

He rewards me with a crooked smile. "Close." He brings his mouth to my ear and whispers, "I want to eat your pussy."

"Hmm. Only if I get to taste you at the same time."

"Deal."

20

PARIS

I'VE NEVER GOTTEN into position so fast as I do with Vanessa. I lie on my back and grab her hips while she hovers above me. Like any guy, I love a sixty-nine, but I can't say I had many of those during my too-fucking-long previous relationship.

I lick her pussy before she can even get her hand around my cock. I pay attention to her reaction, testing things out to see what she likes best. Her legs begin to shake, telling me I'm doing something right. But when her luscious mouth wraps around me, I forget all about technique and let instinct take over.

I'm wild, out of control. My mind is scrambled. I can't think properly when her mouth feels like I'm actually fucking her pussy. Damn it. My girl is good. My balls are tight, ready to explode. I want to prolong this sweet agony, but Vanessa is merciless. She sucks me harder while massaging my balls, and that's my undoing. I come hard, thrusting my cock deeper into her mouth and grunting against her pussy.

She hasn't climaxed yet, and that's something I have to fix ASAP. I dig my fingers deeper into her hips and alternate between fucking her with my tongue and flicking her clit. She releases my cock and rests her cheek against my hip. Sexy moans escape her lips, and it's not long before she's screaming my name at the top of her lungs. I keep going, stopping only when her legs give out and she collapses next to me.

"Okay, I'm done for now, and we didn't even need the condoms." She laughs.

"Give me a few minutes."

She rolls onto her side and props her head on her hand, elbow on the mattress. "The night is young, and our food is getting cold. There's no hurry."

"True, but any minute that I'm not touching you is a waste."

"You're sweet." She walks her fingers over my thigh, getting closer to my dick.

It begins hardening again. "What did I tell you?"

"Well, if you insist." She sits up and reaches for the one box of condoms that didn't get pushed to the floor.

I link my hands behind my head and watch her get out one foil packet and rip it open. Her gaze meets mine, and a devious grin unfurls on her lips.

"What's up, kitten?" I ask.

She rolls the condom down my shaft and then straddles me. "I'm riding you, cowboy."

I grab her by the hips, positioning her better, but she's the one who guides my cock to her entrance. Even with me wearing protection, her pussy feels fucking amazing. I'm already addicted to my girl, and we've only just begun.

Flattening one hand on my shoulder, she gyrates her pelvis slowly, torturing me in the best possible way. I want to control her movements, make her go faster, but at the same time, I like watching her take charge.

I cup one breast instead and tease her nipple with my

thumb. She closes her eyes and moans while moving her hips faster.

"You like that, babe?" I ask.

"Yes," she hisses.

Her pleasure makes me grow harder. She leans forward, bracing both hands on my shoulders while she rises as high as she can before slamming back into me. She's too far from me though. I want to taste her. I reach for the back of her head and bring her closer so I can claim her mouth. She can't move as fast in this position, but I don't care. I need to kiss her.

She leans back a little and looks into my eyes. My heart beats faster, and it has nothing to do with what we're doing in bed. It feels like it's going to burst out of my chest from pure joy. I cup her cheek, and her eyes go soft.

"What?" she asks.

"Nothing. Just drinking you in."

She caresses my lips with her thumb, which proves to be too much temptation for me. I grab her wrist and suck her finger into my mouth. A shuddering breath whooshes from her open lips, and she tightens around me. We begin to move again —I can't help but piston in and out of her, even though she's on top. The rules are out the window. When it comes to making my girl feel good, I won't play fair.

We're both taken over by desire, lost in a fog of lust as we chase our orgasms. I don't know anymore where I end and she begins. At one point, I flip her over so I can fuck her hard while kissing her senseless. She bites my lower lip before she gasps in pleasure. I follow her a moment later, shaking from head to toe as the release overcomes me.

I'll never get tired of this. Never.

It goes without saying that the take-out food I brought is already cold. To be fair, I could skip dinner and the movie and spend the whole damn night in bed with Vanessa, finding new ways to make her come.

She decides to use her crutches in the house again, after I offered to carry her everywhere. An offer that was self-serving, because I'll take any opportunity to touch her. It seems that, now that I've allowed my feelings for her to come to the surface, I want to compensate for all the years I pretended they weren't there.

In the kitchen her attention zeroes in on the food containers, but I nudge her toward the high stool. "You sit your pretty tush there while I warm up dinner, honey."

"How housewifey of you, darling." She smirks.

She still has the glow of someone who was properly fucked, and my plan is for her to always have that post-O-town look. It's crazy how I went from wanting to remain unattached for years after Lydia to thinking of ways I could see Vanessa every day. We both have crazy schedules, so the likelihood of that being possible is slim.

"Do you need anything?" she asks, bringing me back to the here and now.

"What?"

"You have a dazed look on your face, as if you're lost. The plates are in the cupboard behind you."

Shit. I didn't realize I spaced out. "Yeah, plates would be helpful."

I focus on getting the food ready and try not to let my mind wander again. There's no point worrying about things that we can figure out as we go.

"This is surreal," she pipes up.

I glance at her with an eyebrow raised. "What is?"

"You standing half-naked in the middle of my kitchen, prepping dinner."

My lips curl into a crooked smile. "I'm only half-naked because you made me put on my jeans."

"And that was me compromising. Do you know how tempting it is to watch you move around without a shirt on?"

I face her and give her an unobstructed view of the goods. Her eyelids drop a little as fire crackles to life in her gaze. The attention makes me grow hard again, and I forget about dinner.

"If you keep looking at me like that, I'll bend you over that counter and have my way with you."

She stretches her arms over the hard surface and bends forward like a cat, giving me a better view of her glorious tits. "Is that so?"

"Don't tempt me, kitten," I growl.

"Oh, I'm not tempting you. I'm daring you."

I set the plate in my hand near the sink and reach her in three long strides. She lets out a little squeak when I pick her up from the stool and do exactly what I promised—bend her over the counter. Keeping one hand flat against her back, I unzip my jeans.

"I shouldn't have let you convince me to put these back on," I tell her.

"The important thing here is that *I* didn't."

I spread her legs before shoving my hand under her long T-shirt. *Motherfucker.* She's not wearing underwear. I lean forward, pressing my chest against her back, while I bring my lips to her ear and my fingers play with her wet pussy.

"You're one filthy kitten," I whisper.

She moans, "If I'm filthy, it's your fault."

Her reply is like a shot of libido down my cock. I like the idea that I'm the only one who turns her on like this. I shove my hand in my front pocket and fish out the condom I put in there, then ease back so I can get it on as fast as I can.

Vanessa looks over her shoulder and laughs. "You have a condom?"

"It pays to be prepared, babe." I roll the protection down my shaft, and then make her lie flat over the counter once more. "About your dare—last chance to change your mind."

"Never."

"That's my girl." I slam into her, sheathing myself to the hilt, and the world ceases to exist again.

21

VANESSA

EVEN IF I hadn't sprained my ankle, I still wouldn't be able to walk properly. Paris fucked me so good last night that my legs and hips hurt. I even got a bruise, which had never happened before. He wasn't happy about that. I, however, don't care one bit. The little ache is worth all the mind-blowing orgasms he gave me.

Letting him walk out of the house this morning was hard. He looked so delicious, and one morning quickie wasn't enough. Unfortunately, we can't live in our bubble forever.

Paris offered me a ride to campus, but since no one is supposed to know we're dating, I refused. Besides, with the way we can't keep our hands off each other, we were bound to stop halfway to fuck in the back seat of his truck.

I'm showered and ready to go, but the text I sent Heather earlier asking if she'd be able to drive me went unanswered. I'm going to be late if I don't get moving, so I pull up the Uber app. I hate depending on people for anything—especially my sister.

She collects favors and loves to cash in at the most inconvenient times. I'm one second away from requesting a ride when she walks in.

I lift my face from the phone, ready to bitch about her radio silence, when I notice her expression. Her eyes are puffy and red. Heather never cries about anything, so her look *could* be attributed to allergies. But...

"What happened to you?" I ask.

"Nothing." Her reply is clipped, and she doesn't meet my stare.

Hell, maybe she's upset. She continues toward her room, still avoiding eye contact.

"Did you and Leo have a fight?"

She stops and looks over her shoulder. "No. Stop being so nosy."

I sigh. "Fine. Don't tell me. Can you give me a ride to school, or should I call an Uber?"

She turns to me, putting her hands on her hips. "Why can't your boyfriend drive you?"

"Because we don't want people to know we're dating. Did we not have this conversation already?"

She purses her lips before replying. "What time do you have to be on campus?"

"In half an hour."

"Yeah, whatever, I'll drive you. I just need a quick shower." She disappears down the hallway, leaving me perplexed. Since when can Heather get ready in less than half an hour?

I should tell her I'll request a car, but now I'm curious about what's going on with her. And a little concerned.

A ping on my phone alerts me to an incoming message. It's Paris, saying he misses me already. A broad smile blossoms on my lips, but it's erased just as quickly when another message pops up, this one from Ryan, asking if we can grab lunch today.

My blood runs cold from just thinking about the idea of

spending any time with the asshole. But then rage erupts in the pit of my stomach, leaving me shaking. How dare he contact me? I type back furiously.

ME: Not in this lifetime, or next.

When I see the three dots appear, my stomach twists into knots, making me queasy. I block him before he can send his message through. Then I set the phone on the counter, and I fucking lose it. Tears roll down my cheeks, and I can't stop the flood. I didn't react this poorly when I bumped into him, so why does a simple text have this effect on me?

"Vanessa? Why are you crying?" Heather asks as she comes into the kitchen.

Shit. I so didn't want her to see me like this.

I wipe the moisture off my face. "Nothing."

"Bullshit. You wouldn't be bawling your eyes out like that for no reason. Did something happen with Paris? Did he dump you?"

"What?" I squeak. "No. Why would you say that?"

"Because I can't think of any other bad news that would put you in that pitiful state."

I open my mouth to offer an angry retort, but she's not wrong. If Paris dumped me, I'd be devastated. Which is crazy because, until we're out in the open, I don't feel like I'm his girlfriend. That thought makes me sad. In a strange way, it distracts me from the reason I was crying.

"Well, you're wrong."

She crosses her arms and gives me the *I'm going to beat the truth out of you no matter what* look. "Then what happened?"

I was determined to keep Ryan's assault a secret, but maybe my reaction has to do with the fact that no one save Paris knows. I don't want to tell any of my friends on the team, because I feel ashamed that it happened. I'm their captain—I'm supposed to be their role model, the strongest Raven. I definitely don't want to be reminded that Paris witnessed the whole thing. It's a source of immense mortification for me.

I know it's crazy to think like that. Why am I embarrassed about something that was done *to* me? What a great psychologist I'll be one day. That weasel Ryan is the one who should be ashamed. Instead, he's walking around campus with the same arrogant air. He's texting me as if nothing happened.

"Ryan tried to rape me after I broke up with him," I blurt out.

Heather stands there like a statue for a couple of beats. No blinking, no widening of her eyes, no reaction whatsoever. It's no wonder her nickname since high school is Ice Queen.

"When?" she asks finally.

"The day before Lorena's wedding."

Her eyebrows furrow. "That's when Paris came over."

Unable to withstand her detached stare, I look away. "Yeah. He stopped Ryan. Would have beat the shit out of him if I hadn't intervened."

"Why?" Her voice rises an octave.

"Why what?"

"Why did you stop Paris?"

"Because I didn't want him to get in trouble because of that asshole. He wanted to kill Ryan."

"And with reason!" She throws her hands in the air. "I think I'd have killed him myself."

Her admission shocks me. "You would?"

"Why are you surprised? In fact, I'm curious why you didn't rip Ryan's nut sack off yourself."

I blink as I process her words. "No ripping, but I kicked him there. Hard."

"That's something. Did you report him to the police?"

My shoulders sag as I let out a heavy sigh. I shake my head. "I don't want to be known as the girl who was almost raped by her boyfriend."

Glowering, Heather puts her hands on her hips. "You'd rather let a rapist walk free so he can do the same to another girl? Most likely there won't be a Paris around to save them."

Hell. Heather is making me feel like shit. No wonder I didn't want to tell anyone.

"I wasn't thinking about anyone but myself, okay? Yes, that makes me selfish, but fuck, I was just trying to survive," I retort angrily.

"Survive?" Her eyebrows arch. "You've been acting like nothing happened, happy as can be with your new boyfriend."

"Who are you to judge me? You have no idea what it was like for me, how hard it still is. Until you've been in my shoes—"

"I've been in your shoes!" she yells, turning red and sounding out of breath.

My heart skips a beat and then jams hard against my rib cage. "What?"

Her eyes widen as she realizes she blurted out a confession she probably didn't mean to. "Never mind." She begins to turn, but I jump off my high stool and grab her arm.

"Heather." I take a deep breath and loosen my hold. "When were you assaulted?"

She won't look at me, but I can feel her arm tremble.

"It happened a long time ago. It doesn't matter now."

My stomach coils tightly, making me want to hurl. "How long ago?" I whisper.

"Freshman year of high school." She wipes the corners of her eyes.

I release her arm then and stand in front of her. "Who?"

She finally meets my stare. "I don't know. I went to a party, and someone spiked my drink. I woke up alone in a strange bed, my underwear was gone, and there were bloodstains on my inner thighs. So you see, I *couldn't* bring the asshole who raped me to justice, because I don't know who he was. But you can make sure Ryan never pulls that shit again, and you're choosing to let him walk free."

I'm crying again as my heart shatters into a million pieces. "You never told anyone what happened?"

"I told Mom, and she urged me to keep it a secret. You know, for the same bullshit reason you just gave me. She didn't want me to carry the stigma of being a rape victim like it was a scarlet letter."

"I'm so sorry."

I feel like an idiot for saying that. Ryan didn't succeed, and he still made me feel dirty and unworthy. Heather was actually violated, and all I have to say to her is *sorry*.

"Yeah, me too. You know what, I think you should call that Uber after all." She veers toward the hallway.

"I don't need to go. I can stay with you."

"No. You're the last person I want around me right now."

Her comment feels like a punch to my chest. I want to curl into a ball and cry some more. But I have to respect Heather's wish to be alone. She gave me the house so I could spend time with Paris. The least I can do is offer her the same courtesy.

22

VANESSA

I SHOULD HAVE ASKED the Uber driver to take me anywhere but campus. Going to class was pointless. I couldn't concentrate, couldn't hold a conversation for more than a few seconds before I spaced out. I kept replaying Heather's confession in my head, and the guilt in my chest festered like a disease. I can't believe I never noticed anything in high school. Was I so caught up in my own drama with Paris that I failed to see what she was going through? She's my twin. I should have sensed that something terrible had happened to her.

The morning goes by in a blur, and by the time lunch rolls around, I'm ready to get the fuck out of there. I have no idea where I'm going, but it's definitely better than staying and pretending I'm not falling apart.

It's not until I pull my phone out to call an Uber that I see all the missed text messages and a couple of phone calls from Paris. There are also messages from Sadie, and a few other team members. Hell. I don't want to talk to anyone, not even through texting.

What I need is to gather the courage to report Ryan, but every time I think about it, the fear that no one will believe me keeps me in a choke hold. Paris would need to testify, a whole circus would form, and the personal details of my life would be cut open and dissected. I don't think I can solve this one alone. I probably should make an appointment to talk to a therapist. I *will* make one.

That decision makes me feel a little bit better. As for my teammates, I can blow them off for a few more hours, but I don't want to do that to Paris. What we have is too new, and he could mistake my radio silence as a sign that I'm no longer interested in dating him. I don't want to lose him again.

I scroll through his texts. They're sweet at first, but then, they grow worried. He didn't leave me any voice messages though. I stop near a bench and prop my crutches against it, then start a reply.

I don't get further than a couple of words before my phone is yanked from my hands. "What the fu—" The swear word gets lodged in my throat when I see it's Ryan who fucking stole my phone.

"Who are you texting, darling?"

"Give me my phone back, asshole." I step forward and wince when I put all my weight on my bad foot. At this rate, I'll never get cleared to play soccer.

I don't get the phone back, and I can tell from Ryan's furious expression that he's read most of the texts Paris sent me.

"That's why you fucking blocked me, bitch? You're screwing that meathead? How long has it been going on?"

"Fuck you, Ryan. I don't owe you any explanations. Give me my damn phone!" I reach for his hand and try to yank it free, but he shoves me so hard that I stagger back and, thanks to having only one good foot, I fall and hit my face against the metal bench.

White-hot pain flares across my cheek, and for a dizzying moment the world flickers to black. My ears are ringing, but I can still hear the sound of shouting.

A moment later, a stranger drops into a crouch in front of me. "Are you okay?"

"I don't know." I touch my cheek and find it wet.

"You have a cut there," he says. "Here, I got your phone back."

"Thanks."

"Can you stand up?"

I wish I could say yes, but I'm light-headed as fuck. Now that I've regained focus, I look over his shoulder and search for Ryan. He's gone, which is too bad, because he deserves to be punched in the throat.

"I may need assistance," I tell him.

He pulls me up and immediately steps back. I appreciate his effort to make sure he doesn't overstep. I pay attention to him. He's young, probably a freshman, and on the scrawny side. I wonder if he was the one who yelled at Ryan.

"Thanks for intervening," I say.

"Of course. I thought he was your friend at first, acting like an idiot, or I would have butted in sooner."

"He's an asshole. I'm surprised he didn't start anything with you."

"Too many witnesses." He nods his head toward a spot behind me.

I turn and see the crowd that's beginning to disperse. "And yet, you were the only one who helped."

"I think someone else would have, too. I was just the fastest."

"Well, thank you for the assist. I'm not usually this pathetic, but I'm not in top shape currently." I point at my foot.

"Yeah, which makes his actions even worse. You probably should take care of that cut. I can walk with you to the medical building."

As much as I appreciate the offer, I don't want him to witness me having another meltdown. I was barely holding it together already, and Ryan had to show up to fuck me up even more.

I search for a tissue in my backpack, and then dab the wound. "It's okay. I can get there on my own. What's your name?"

"Philip Meester. You're Vanessa Castro, right? The Ravens' midfielder."

God, I wish he hadn't recognized me. "Yup. Nice to meet you, Philip. I'd better get going."

"Uh, do you want to report Ryan Watergate to campus police? What he did wasn't cool."

My eyebrows shoot to the heavens. "You know Ryan?"

Philip looks a little guilty, and I don't understand his reaction. "Yeah. I met him during rush week. I ended up joining the Pikes, though."

Shit. That means he knows Leo, Heather's boyfriend, since Leo's the president of that fraternity. That also means Philip probably knows that Ryan is my ex.

"I'll deal with Ryan later," I say.

He stares at me a beat too long and then says, "I hope you do. I'll back you up if needed. Take care, Vanessa."

I watch him leave, and I wonder if there is a hidden meaning behind his comment. It's almost as if he knows more stuff about Ryan than what he witnessed a moment ago.

The sting on my face snaps me out of my musings, and it also serves as a wake-up call. I have to report Ryan. Not to the campus police though. They'll involve the school administration, and *they'll* do anything they can to smooth things over and avoid a scandal. The school's reputation took a hit when Nick Fowler, a former soccer player at Rushmore, posted a sexist list that included all female athletes.

The sting from the cut doesn't burn as much, but even if it's superficial, it's bleeding a lot. Instead of going to see a nurse, I head into the first restroom I come across and try to stop the blood flow. The cut is minimal, but my cheek is swollen from the impact.

I think about what Heather told me, and how our mother reacted. Would she have told Heather to keep quiet if she knew who her rapist was? It's hard to tell with Mom. She's so focused on appearances though, hence why she created all that drama after the stolen wine incident. She wanted to make sure there was no doubt Paris was the one who tried to corrupt me.

Shit. Paris. I never texted him back. How am I going to explain my messed-up face? I don't know how he'll react, even if I say I'm ready to report Ryan. He might do something to that bastard first.

Maybe I should just tell him I fell. It's a miracle he hasn't gone after Ryan yet. If he knows how I got my new injury, he might do something that for sure will fuck up his future. I can't have that on my conscience.

I clean up the blood and then grab a new paper towel and dry off my face. I go through several until I'm confident I don't look like an extra from a slasher movie, and then I head out.

It's just my luck that the man I need but should avoid right now finds me before I can get the cut taken care of. Paris's face is closed off at first—a sign that he was already thinking the worst about my silence. But when his attention shifts to the cut on my cheek, he goes from serious to concerned in zero point one second.

He reaches me in a couple of long strides, stopping short of invading my space completely. "Kitten, what happened?"

"I... uh, I fell." The lie feels bitter on my tongue, but I'm doing this to protect him.

"You fell? How?"

"I'm not really sure. I tripped and hit my face on a bench. I'm on my way to the infirmary."

He's watching me closely, almost as if he doesn't believe me. I never lie, so it's no surprise I'm terrible at it. My body is trembling, and my heart is beating so fast, it's hard to believe he can't hear the thumping.

Before he can see the deception on my face, I say, "I'm sorry I never replied to you. It's been nonstop for me this morning, and when I finally had a break, this happened." I point at my cheek.

His expression softens. "I was a little worried, if I'm honest. I did blow up your phone. I thought that maybe you..." He rubs the back of his neck, looking sheepish.

The adorable expression makes me feel even guiltier about lying to him. I want to kiss him and forget that I'm being a total bitch for not telling him the truth. But he was the one who wanted to keep our relationship a secret for now, so I don't dare any PDA.

Although... Ryan already knows I'm dating Paris. Pretty soon the news will be across the entire campus and, knowing that piece of shit, he's going to spin a story that will make me look bad. He was already insinuating that I was screwing Paris before I broke up with him. I'm running out of time. I need to go to the police, but I don't think I can bring Paris with me. No, I have to do this on my own.

"You thought that I what?" I ask.

"That you changed your mind about us."

A knot forms in my chest. The vulnerability in his tone makes me want to be truthful with him about something at least, even if it's going to blow up in my face.

"I won't change my mind. I've been in love with you since we were thirteen."

He doesn't speak for a beat, just stares at me. But then

laughter bubbles up his throat. He shakes his head, and I feel like an idiot.

"Okay, then. I'd better go now and find a hole to hide in." I make a motion to circle around him, but he raises his arm, and blocks my path.

"You're not going anywhere, kitten." He steps into my space, snaking his strong arms around my waist. "Not until I kiss you." He leans down and presses his lips softly against mine.

I melt into his embrace, wanting more than an innocent peck on the lips, but Paris eases off before I can attack his mouth. "Come on. Let's get that boo-boo taken care of."

"Okay," I reply dreamily, forgetting for a moment that we aren't thirteen anymore.

I wish that we were.

23

PARIS

"Ugh, I look hideous." Vanessa touches the bandage on her cheek.

I peel my eyes away from the road to glance at her. "You look as beautiful as always, kitten."

"How can you say that? The right side of my face is twice as big as the left."

"You'd look gorgeous even if your entire head was a giant watermelon."

She twists her expression into an exaggerated scowl, making me laugh. It sucks that she got hurt, but I'm still riding the high of her confession. She said she's been in love with me since we were kids—pretty much as long as I've been in love with her. I have yet to confess though, and as much as I wanted to say the words right then, it didn't feel right professing my love when she had a bleeding cut on her face.

"You're just saying that to get laid."

"I'm not!" I retort, fighting the urge to laugh again.

She grows quiet, making me curious. I chance another look and find her facing the window.

I cover her hand with mine. "What's wrong, kitten?"

"Nothing. Can we go to your place instead of mine? I mean, if that's okay?"

"Of course it's okay. Although, I have to head to practice in an hour."

"Shit. I forgot you have a life besides coming to my rescue."

I bring our joined hands to my lips and kiss the top of hers. "Being your knight in shining armor is my number one priority, sweetheart."

Her eyebrows furrow. "I'm not a damsel in distress."

Damn, and here I thought I was being romantic with my comment. I didn't realize how sexist it was.

"I know you aren't. You're a fierce warrior, but even the most badass heroes can use help from time to time."

She narrows her eyes. "Nice save."

"So, why can't you go home? I mean, not that I don't love the idea of you in my bed, but I live with three loud and messy dudes."

"Yeah, I'm aware of that. Heather asked for the house. Since she did me a solid yesterday, I can't deny her the favor. But if you don't want your roommates to know about us, I can call one of my teammates."

"Are you crazy? You're staying with me. I thought I made my point when I kissed you in front of everyone earlier."

"Well, there weren't a lot of people around us then."

"Trust me, all it takes is one person for the rest of Rushmore to know."

"Why? Because you're on the football team?"

This sounds like a trap, so I'd better tread carefully. I know the Ravens aren't happy that the football team gets tons of perks from the school administration while they have to fight for everything, even though they're one of the best college soccer teams in the country.

"Well, yeah. And I'm not saying that because I'm cocky."

"I know you aren't."

"Do you need to stop by your house to pack an overnight bag?" I change the subject before we plunge deeper into a topic that's political and unpleasant.

"Nah, I can sleep in one of your T-shirts."

"Or you can sleep wearing nothing at all." I wink.

She runs a hand through her hair and pulls a section over her face to hide the bandage. "I have a better idea. I can wear your T-shirt over my head so you don't have to look at this hideousness."

"Hmm. I think you're fishing for compliments, kitten."

"Now you're confusing me with my twin."

A random song comes through the speakers, and Vanessa reaches for the volume dial. "I love this one."

"Who sings this?" I ask. "Justin Timberlake?"

"Oh my god. Who *are* you? How can you not know 'I Want It That Way'? It's a Backstreet Boys classic!"

"You expect me to know songs by a nineties boy band? I wasn't even born."

"Okay, fine. This song came out in 1999. But it was featured in one of my favorite shows of all time."

"I'm going out on a limb here and saying it's not a fantasy series." I smirk.

"Duh. *Brooklyn 99.* It's a hilarious cop show."

"I think I've heard of it. You can introduce it to me when I get back from practice. Although I might have other things in mind." I run a hand up her thigh, but she bats it away before I reach her pussy.

"I don't feel sexy, so Jake Peralta will have to be your consolation prize."

I wrinkle my nose. "Yeah, like I want a dude replacing my hot-as-sin girlfriend."

"I'm your girlfriend?" The surprise in her voice is authentic, but it shouldn't be. Hell, maybe I didn't make myself clear yesterday.

I'm glad I have to stop at a red light so I can reply to her while looking into her eyes. "Yes. Did you have any doubt about that?"

"I wasn't sure." She shrugs. "Maybe it has to do with the fact we weren't broadcasting our relationship to the world yet."

Guilt pierces my chest like an iron spear, making me regret ever asking her to keep us a secret. She didn't want to do it at first, and now I know she changed her mind because she loves me.

"I'm sorry. I was an idiot for wanting to hide that you're my girl."

A blaring car horn warns me I'm holding up traffic. Reluctantly, I switch my attention to the road and miss her reaction to my statement.

A moment passes before she says, "I never thought I'd confess this, but I love hearing you call me *your girl*. It's even better than being your girlfriend."

"Get used to it then, kitten. You were always my girl. I just lost sight of you for a while."

She doesn't reply, and I'm afraid I said something wrong. In my peripheral vision, I see her wipe the corner of her eye.

"Babe, are you crying?"

"What? No." She looks out the window as she sinks into the truck seat.

I turn on the blinker and park in the first spot I find, which is in front of an empty store with a For Rent sign.

"Is this where you live?" she asks.

"No." I unbuckle my seat belt and pinch her chin to turn

her face to mine. "You know you don't need to hide anything from me, right, kitten?"

Her eyes go rounder. "I'm not hiding anything."

"I made you cry. I'm sorry."

She shakes her head. "It's nothing. I'm just overly emotional these days. It's probably PMS."

"You have reason to be, even if it's not PMS." I cup her cheek. "I'm here for you. Always. I love you."

Her breathing hitches. Then her eyes become brighter and rounder. She looks away, covering her face with her hands. Her body starts to shake, so I free her from the constraints of her seat belt and pull her into a hug. A ragged sob escapes her lips, but I refrain from saying a word. I let her cry for as long as she needs, her face pressed against my chest.

I suspected she was putting on a brave face in front of me, and like an idiot, I pretended she was fine. But she isn't, not by any stretch of the imagination, and I'm certain it all comes back to the evening she was attacked. I need to do something. That son of a bitch can't remain unpunished. But using brute force isn't the way to go, even if I'd love nothing more than to give him the ass kicking of his life.

I need to find another way to make him pay.

24

VANESSA

PARIS'S ROOMMATES aren't home when we finally make it there. His apartment is on campus, not far from where Andreas and Danny live. The building is similar, with its red brick exterior and modern industrial style. The apartment itself is spacious, with a big open kitchen and living room. There's even an area where they managed to fit a foosball table. Any other day, I'd want to play.

"Welcome to *minha casa*," he says.

Despite feeling wretched, I crack a smile. "Are you learning to speak Portuguese?"

He pulls me into his arms and kisses me on the cheek. "I'd do anything for you, kitten."

"I know. I feel the same way about you. So... should I learn to speak Greek?"

He eases off and when I look up, I catch his exaggerated scowl. "You know I don't speak Greek, right?"

"What? The smartest kid in All Saints never learned the language of his people?"

"Mock me all you want. Unlike your folks, my parents didn't make Cory and me learn. They were too concerned about what the neighbors would say if they heard us speaking a foreign language."

"That's too bad. I can't wait to speak Portuguese with you in front of them. Your mother will have a cow." I laugh.

"Probably, if she doesn't die of a heart attack when you come to my game on Saturday."

Oh crap. His first game of the season. I forgot about it. I must make a face, because his eyebrows furrow.

"You're coming, right?" he asks.

"I... I don't know. The Ravens also play on Saturday, and I need to be there."

He closes his eyes for a moment and shakes his head. "Of course. I'm an idiot. Don't mind me."

"Let me know the time. Maybe I can make it to both."

"All right." An alarm beeps, and it's coming from his pocket. He pulls his cell phone out and curses. "Shit. I have to go, kitten. Are you going to be okay?"

"Yeah. Don't worry about me."

"There's food in the fridge. Help yourself to anything you want."

I nod. "I'll be all right. Go. I don't want you to be late because of me."

"Hold on, let me give you a tour of the apartment first."

He takes my hand and veers toward the hallway. "The first door to your right is James Parker's room. He's one of the Rebels' new recruits."

"Yeah, I've seen him around."

"Nice guy, but messy as hell. Don't go in there if chaos makes your skin crawl."

I wrinkle my nose. "How bad is it?"

"Bad." He laughs, and then points at the door to our left. "This is Mark and Doug Ronson's room."

"Brothers?"

"Cousins. One is premed like me, and the other is studying computer science."

"Gotcha. Brainiacs like you."

"I'm not a brainiac," he grumbles.

I snort. "Sure you aren't."

"Anyway, this is my room." He opens the last door at the end of the hallway.

It's a big space with a massive wall-to-wall window that offers a great view of campus. The king-size bed is set against a black wall with chalk scribbles all over it.

"What's that?"

"Oh, that's my brainstorm wall. I turned it into a blackboard so I can doodle, write notes..."

I squint, "Draw dick pics..."

"What?" He walks closer and curses. "Those Ronson fuckers." He tries to wipe off the drawing with his fingers, but all that does is make it blurry.

"Was that supposed to be a picture of *your* dick? Because if it was, they got the size seriously wrong."

He looks at me and smirks. "That they did."

His dimples make an appearance, and I melt. I love when he smiles at me like that. He walks over and pulls me against his solid chest. Then he kisses me quickly on the lips before stepping back. "Hell, I wish I didn't have to go to practice."

"Yeah, me too. I'll be here when you get back though."

"That's something to look forward to." He kisses me again and then almost bolts out the door, taking all the happiness with him.

My heart becomes heavy again, as if it's made of steel. I'm suddenly bone tired, so I just stay in his bedroom. I was supposed to see the team's trainer today, but I told her I wasn't feeling well and rescheduled for tomorrow. There's no chance I'll make it to the police station today either. I haven't changed my mind, but I have to be stronger mentally to face something I know will be brutal to my mental health.

I'm a mess, a veritable yarn ball of guilt. I'm letting my team down by not showing up for my checkup, by not answering their messages. I thought I was stronger. I thought I could forget about what Ryan did to me and move on with my life. But things aren't that simple. Whether I like it or not, that bastard left a permanent mark on my soul. Heather's confession didn't help either. My guilt for not reporting him has doubled, despite the fact I've decided to rectify that.

Alone in Paris's bedroom, I cry again. It seems that's all I can do today. I've taken enough psychology classes to know that crying is part of the healing process, but all it does is make me feel weak and pathetic. I thought I was a badass, but maybe I'm a meek damsel in distress after all.

I end up falling asleep, and when I wake up, I see that it's past seven p.m. I stay curled up in Paris's bed though, not having the energy to move. I bring my nose to his pillow because it smells like him, a mix of nutmeg, sandalwood, and leather. It does give me some comfort, but my chest feels hollow, and it seems I'll never be happy again. God, now I'm having emo thoughts. What's wrong with me?

The front door opens, and male voices warn me that two of Paris's roommates are home. I knew that the new guy on the team was rooming with him, but I had no clue who the other two were. It isn't like I kept tabs on who was in Paris's life. I was aware mostly of his relationship with Lydia, and as much as I tried to tell myself I didn't care, the sight of them together always made my heart bleed slowly and steadily.

Since I'm no longer alone in the apartment, there's zero chance I'm going to venture into the living room. I'm glad that Paris has an en suite and I don't need to go out there to use the restroom. My stomach feels empty, but I can survive without eating. I'm not sure I can keep anything down anyway.

I look at my phone just as a message flashes on the screen. It's Sadie, asking if I'm okay. I type a quick reply, partially lying once again. Then I flip my phone down so I can't see her answer and feel worse about my deceit.

I force myself out of bed to use the bathroom. It's spotless, which is a relief. Guys can be pigs. When I catch my reflection in the mirror, I wince. It's no surprise that I look like a witch, with tangled hair and dark circles under my eyes. The swelling on my face has lessened, but the area is bruising. I can't wait too long to report Ryan. I need the evidence that he hurt me. And Paris will find out I lied to him today.

God, what a fucking mess I made. My eyes prickle as the urge to cry renews.

I bite the inside of my cheek to try to stop the waterworks, and then I search for a hairbrush.

Instead, I find a pink hair band. I step back, shoving the drawer shut fast, as if there were a snake in there. What else has Lydia left behind? I don't want to succumb to retroactive jealousy, but that's exactly what's happening now.

"Kitten?" Paris calls from the room.

Shit. He's back, and I'm on the verge of losing my mind again. He already saw me fall apart once today. I don't want him to think I'm breakable.

"I'll be right out." I finger-comb my hair, since I didn't find a brush. It's not much of an improvement, but better than nothing.

When I walk out of the bathroom, he's sitting on the edge of the bed. His face splits into a broad smile, making my heart beat a little faster. The darkness swirling in my chest loses strength.

"How are you feeling?" he asks.

"Much better now."

I walk over with the intention of sitting next to him. But he pulls me onto his lap and kisses me so sweetly that I might develop an addiction. Who am I kidding? I'm already addicted to him. I melt into his embrace, taking solace in his warmth and strength.

"I missed you," he whispers against my lips.

"I missed you too."

He eases back and looks into my eyes. "I'm going to sound cheesy as hell, but I can't believe that you're actually here. It feels like a dream."

Hearing the man I love tell me that, it's impossible not to melt. But at the same time, this moment feels bittersweet. There's a burden in my chest, the lie I told him weighing heavily on my conscience.

Before he can read my soul's torment in my gaze, I pinch his arm playfully.

"Ouch. What was that for?" he asks.

"To prove you aren't dreaming."

He narrows his eyes. "Oh, you're playing with fire, kitten."

In a blur, I go from sitting on his lap to flat on my back with Paris on top of me.

"What are you doing?" I ask through a laugh.

"There are other less painful ways to prove that I'm not dreaming." He nuzzles my neck, sending goose bumps down my arm.

"You're one horny dude, aren't you?"

Resting on his forearms, he leans back. "That's what happens when I have a girlfriend who looks like you. I can't help myself."

I knit my brows together. "Your girlfriend doesn't look too hot right now."

"Tell that to my cock." He gyrates his hips, pressing his erection against my core.

Humming, I close my eyes. "Okay, I'll pretend I believe you."

"Believe me, kitten. No one has ever put my libido into overdrive like you do."

"Like you have so many to compare with me," I blurt out, then regret my words immediately when I see the constricted look on his face.

He rolls off me onto his back and stares at the ceiling. Shit. I should have kept my mouth shut.

Leaning on my elbow, I say, "I shouldn't have said that. I'm sorry."

"I'm actually glad that you did." He looks at me. "I didn't know how else to talk about it without sounding like an ass."

"I don't follow."

He sighs. "Lydia wasn't my first."

"Oh." Several emotions compete to take over my heart. I'm jealous of whoever "initiated" him, but I'm also glad it wasn't that manipulative bitch.

"Yeah. I knew she wanted to be more than friends, and I wasn't sure if that was what I wanted. The summer before freshman year, I went to visit my family in Greece, and that's when I lost my virginity to some random girl I met at a party."

"Do you even remember her name?"

He grimaces. "Will you think less of me if I say that I don't?"

"Uh, yes and no. I mean, I'm glad you don't remember, because it means she doesn't have any hold on you."

He caresses my cheek with the back of his hand. "Kitten, only you have a hold on me."

"Good. So does that mean you only slept with two girls besides me?"

"Ehhh..."

My jaw drops. "You dog! How many girls did you screw in Greece?"

"Oh, just the one, and only once. The others came later."

My heart constricts painfully. He started dating Lydia at the beginning of freshman year. That memory is imprinted on my mind, because the sight of them holding hands obliterated me. I never pegged Paris as the unfaithful type, and even if he cheated on that viper, it doesn't sit well with me.

"Don't give me that look. I didn't cheat on Lydia."

Relief washes over me, but more questions pop into my head. "You've been inseparable since you started dating."

"Not exactly. We were getting too serious too fast, and I freaked out. On spring break that year, I broke up with her. That's when the other girls came into the picture, but before you call me a dog again, there were only two."

"And then you went right back to that witch."

"Yeah. Not the smartest decision I ever made."

I rub the space between his brows, trying to smooth the lines there. "It's over now. She'll never come near you again if I have anything to say about it."

He cracks a smile, and his eyes dance with glee. "Oh, what are you going to do, kitten? Fight over me?"

"If it comes to that, hell yes. You're mine, Andino." I straddle him. "Don't forget that."

"Hmm, I think you'd better remind me with actions."

I lean forward, touching his nose with mine. "Are you daring me?"

"You betcha."

25

PARIS

I wish I could have played chauffeur for Vanessa this morning, but Coach Clarkson wanted us on the field bright and early, so I dropped her off at her place before heading to practice. At least I was able to keep my mind on the game, but that didn't mean I wasn't counting the minutes until I got to see her again.

I've never felt impatient like this before. Lydia was my only previous serious girlfriend, and truth be told, she never made me feel this way. I thought I loved her, but now that I'm out of that relationship, I'm realizing I mistook gratitude for love, and then it morphed into guilt.

"Good practice today, Andino," Danny says, running a hand over his long hair. "I'm glad to see your mind was one hundred percent in the game."

"Yes. I'm back, bro."

Most of the guys have left the locker room, something I notice when Danny grows serious.

My spine becomes taut, and I have an idea why he waited

until we were practically alone to come talk to me. "You have something on your mind."

"Am I that transparent?"

"Yeah, don't ever play poker."

He chuckles. "You aren't the first person to tell me that. Anyway, it's about Vanessa. She's the mystery girl, isn't she?"

I'm surprised it took him until today to figure out I'm dating her.

"Yes."

"You don't have to worry. I won't say a word about what you told me. But... hell, now I want to punch the shit out of that son of a bitch even more."

His comment ignites the fury that's been simmering in my gut since I was denied the same. "Join the club, bro."

"If doing something to him wouldn't mess up your life, I wouldn't stand in your way."

I clap his shoulder. "Thanks, man. Coming from you, that's pretty fucking huge."

He squints. "I'm beginning to hate this reputation I have that I don't lose my temper."

"I'm just saying, you don't act on impulse. That's why you're a badass quarterback."

He crosses his arms. "I suppose that's true. But there are exceptions, and if I were in your shoes, I wouldn't stop to think about the consequences."

"What are you trying to say, Hudson? Do you *want* me to go after Ryan?"

His eyes widen. "No, that's not what I'm saying at all." He shakes his head. "Please don't do anything stupid. Catch you later for lunch?"

"I'm meeting Vanessa at noon in the main cafeteria. You and Sadie are more than welcome to join us."

"Sounds good. Just be warned—I don't think Sadie knows about you and Vanessa yet."

My eyebrows furrow. "How did you hear about it, then?"

"Conrad made a comment earlier. Didn't she spend the night at your place?"

Mental head slap. I'm such an idiot. Conrad is one of my roommates, and he was around when Vanessa and I came out of the bedroom this morning.

"Ah, yeah. I completely forgot I introduced them."

"What happened with not wanting to come out in public yet?"

"I don't want to pretend around her."

I don't get into the specifics about Lydia stealing Vanessa's poem. It's not that I want to keep it a secret, but until I talk to Lydia, it's best if my friends don't know.

He nods. "Do you think Lydia will be a problem?"

"Yeah. But I don't care."

VANESSA

MY PHONE VIBRATES in my pocket, sending my heart aflutter. Sadly, it isn't a message from Paris, but a text from Sadie, whom I've been neglecting.

SADIE: You're a sucky friend. I hate you.

Ah damn. I'd better call her back to find out if she's angry about my silence, or if it's something else.

She answers on the first ring. "Oh, look who's alive."

"I'm sorry. My life has been hectic." Not a lie.

"Yeah, hectic in *Paris's bed.* How could you not tell me you were dating him?" she yells, forcing me to pull the phone away from my ear to avoid hearing damage.

"We decided to keep it on the down-low to avoid drama."

"Since when am I drama? You know I'd have kept your secret!"

Way to make me feel shitty about it, Sadie. My excuse is lame, I know. I was afraid that she'd make me explain how I got together with Paris, and I still can't talk to her about my attack, but for different reasons. She's going to find out after I report Ryan, but hopefully not before the game on Saturday. It's the first of the season, and I need the girls' focus to stay sharp, especially with me out of commission. I can't fuck up our season by dumping my situation on them.

"I'm sorry, okay? It's all so new and unexpected. I wanted to enjoy Paris without the world knowing about us."

"Talk about unexpected. I didn't think you cared much for the guy."

"Well... I've known him since we were kids."

"Shut your face. How come I didn't know that? Oh yeah, because you're an arsehole who tells me nothing."

Shaking my head, I sigh. "How long are you going to stay mad at me?"

"It depends on your groveling. Buuut... you know I can be easily bribed." She laughs.

And just like that, I know that we're good. "A round of drinks on me the next time we go out?"

"Yeah, that should do it. Anyway, when you said you wanted to avoid drama, were you referring to his ex, or yours?"

I snort. Like I care about what that asshole thinks. "Mostly her. How did you find out about Paris anyway?"

"Not from Danny. He'd better not have known before me, or he'll be sorry. He won't get off easily like you did."

I roll my eyes. Sadie and Danny couldn't be more different in terms of personality, and yet, they're perfect for each other. Even her father, Danny's coach, has accepted their relationship as endgame. I know in the beginning it was hard for him to

forget that his QB was screwing his daughter, especially after he
caught them in a compromising position.

"If he does know, he probably only learned about it
recently. Please don't go savage on him. He might not have had
the chance to tell you."

"Don't worry. I'm not going to castrate the boy. I like his dick
too much to do that to him."

A bubble of laughter goes up my throat. "I bet you do. So,
who told you?"

"Eh, you're not going to like it."

I'm about to enter the main building on campus, where the
cafeteria is. I'm meeting Paris there in ten minutes, but I decide
to finish the conversation with Sadie away from eavesdropping
ears.

"Hold on." I tuck my crutches under one arm so I can move
and hold the phone at the same time. Then I change course
and trudge to a nearby tree. "Why?"

"It seems your douche ex posted a video on TikTok
accusing you of cheating on him with Paris. It's gone semiviral."

"That *motherfucker*," I say through clenched teeth.

"Yeah. I blocked his ass after that encounter the other day,
but the girls on the team didn't. I don't think they even know
you broke up with him."

"I blocked him too, and yeah, I should have sent an update
on the group chat."

"But how did that wanker find out?"

I pinch the bridge of my nose, regretting now keeping my
friends in the dark for so long. "I had another confrontation
with the bastard yesterday."

"You have got to be kidding me. What did he do?"

My stomach clenches painfully, making me sick. I don't
want to tell Sadie that he hurt me for the same reason I don't
want her to know about the assault. Damn it. I'm sick and tired
of Ryan fucking with my life.

"Vanessa? Are you still there?" she asks when I take too long to reply. "If that bellend did something to you, I'm going to rip his nut sack off."

"He—"

"You fucking whore!" a woman screams behind me, and I practically jump out of my skin.

I turn to see Lydia marching toward me with murderous intentions flashing in her crazy eyes.

Hell.

"Who's that?" Sadie asks.

"The drama I was trying to avoid. I'll call you later." I put my phone away before Sadie can reply. I need my hands free in case the she-devil wants to get physical. I hope she tries something. If she throws the first punch, I'll have no choice but to defend myself. No one will be able to accuse me of breaking the student code of conduct, and I'll get my revenge. The lying bitch deserves an ass kicking.

Forcing a fake smile, I reply, "Lydia, always a pleasure."

"I *knew* you were trying to take Paris away from me."

My eyebrows shoot to the heavens. "*I* was trying to take Paris from you? Isn't that what you did to me? You know that plagiarism is a crime, right?"

Her eyes bug out. "What are you talking about?"

"Quit the innocent act, honey. Paris and I know that you stole my letter, copied my poem, and claimed you wrote it."

"That's a lie. You're just making up shit to take him from me! I watched the video your ex posted on TikTok. You've been screwing my boyfriend behind my back all this time."

Is this bitch for real?

"*Ex*-boyfriend. And are you really going to stand there and deny you stole my poem?" I laugh in derision. "You are one crazy bitch. I'm glad that Paris is finally aware of how awful you are."

She's not taking my bait, and I'm sick of this conversation. I might end up throwing the first punch if I don't leave. I try to walk around her, but unfortunately, I'm still wearing the ankle brace, and I'm too slow to move.

My only warning that she's snapped is a deranged yell before she tackles me to the ground. The grass softens my fall, but one of the crutches ends up underneath me and pokes into my back. The most dangerous thing is Lydia and her long nails, though. She tries to scratch my face and ends up pulling the bandage off my cut before I can grab her wrists and push her back.

"Get off me!" I yell.

Like a rabid dog, she comes at me again with bared teeth. I barely have time to sit up, much less to pull my arm back to punch her ugly face.

"Lydia, what the hell!" Paris is suddenly there, dragging his ex off me. "Are you insane?"

"Don't touch me!" She struggles against his hold.

Meanwhile, someone else drops into a crouch by my side. "Are you okay?"

It's the freshman who helped me yesterday. Philip Meester. Why is he always around when I'm in distress? Maybe he's a stalker posing as a Good Samaritan. That would be my luck.

"Uh, no."

He helps me up, even though I wish I didn't need his assistance. But I don't think I could get up on my own, even if my ankle wasn't sprained. I'm shaking from head to toe, adrenaline making my heart thump fast inside my chest. I'm pissed that I didn't get a chance to do some damage to Lydia like I wanted to.

Paris is no longer holding her, but she's far from calm. "How could you *do* this to me? I thought you loved me!" she whines.

Oh my god. She's still playing the victim card, even though I told her we know she lied.

"Do *what* to you? We've been broken up for six months, Lydia."

"Don't play dumb with me. I know you were screwing that cunt way before we broke up."

He takes a step forward, pointing a finger in her direction. "You watch your mouth when you talk about Vanessa. The only person here who deserves to be called that awful name is you."

Lydia's face turns bright red, and her jaw drops. "I—I can't believe you said that to me! Do you want me to k—"

He takes a step back, raising his palm. "Don't you *dare* say that. I will *not* fall prey to your manipulations anymore. I cannot be responsible for your actions."

"So you don't care if I die?"

Fuck. Can I punch her now? I can't believe she's doing this to Paris in front of all these witnesses. Of course a bunch of the assholes are recording the scene. I bet someone is broadcasting it live. I fucking hate how social media gives power to scum.

"I'll be sad, but I'm not your therapist or your parent."

Crocodile tears run down her cheeks. "You'll regret your words one day, Paris." She turns and runs away, shoving some onlookers out of her path.

"Wow," Philip says, drawing Paris's attention to him.

His eyebrows furrow, maybe because he doesn't like how close the guy is to me. "Who are you?"

The kid's cheeks flush. "I... uh, my name is Philip Meester."

"How do you know Vanessa?" Paris walks over and draws me closer to him and away from Philip.

Man, it seems this altercation with Lydia dialed up his protective mode to the max.

"I helped her the other day when her ex was giving her trouble."

Oh hell. Shut up, Philip.

Paris tenses. "What did he do?" His hold around my waist tightens.

"He stole her phone, and when she tried to get it back, he pushed her onto a bench. That's how she got that cut." He gestures to my cheek.

Paris turns me around and gazes into my eyes. His own are swimming with the hurt of betrayal. "You said you tripped."

"I'm sorry. I didn't want you to go after Ryan before I had the chance to report him to the police."

Rubbing his face, Paris stares into the distance.

"Paris? Please, look at me."

He does so, and I'm surprised that his eyes aren't brimming with anger as I expected. I lied to him, after all.

The hurt is still there, though.

He pulls me into a tight hug, hiding his face in the crook of my neck. "I'm sorry I wasn't there to protect you from him. I'm sorry that I didn't go after him and make him pay for hurting you the first time."

"Don't apologize. What happened to me wasn't your fault."

"Not the first time, but everything he's done since *is* my fault. I'll make it right, kitten. I promise."

I pull back and capture his gaze. "You're not going after him. Please tell me that isn't what you're planning to do."

He caresses my cheek gently, then gives me a peck on the lips. "Don't worry about it, kitten. Let's go home."

26

VANESSA

Paris drops me off at my place, but he doesn't linger, not even after I beg him to come inside. I look out the window and watch him leave with tears in my eyes. He swore he wasn't angry with me for lying, but my heart tells me otherwise. I didn't trust him. Now the guilt is consuming me.

Heather walks into the living room. "What happened this time?"

Wiping my cheeks, I turn around. "Fucking Ryan happened."

Her face is a cold mask as she studies me. "Are you talking about the TikTok video?"

"You've seen it?"

"I don't think there's a soul on campus that hasn't seen it. What happened to your face?"

Shit, I forgot that Heather didn't see me yesterday. I touch the cut, which, mercifully, Lydia didn't rip open again. "Ryan."

Heather's blue eyes turn as dark as a stormy sky. "He did that to you? When?"

"Yesterday. He stole my phone while I was texting Paris and found out about us. When I tried to get my phone back, he pushed me. I fell and hit my face on a bench."

"And you still didn't report him?" Heather's voice rises, and I wince.

"I didn't have a chance, okay? I'm going to, but I was a fucking mess yesterday, and then Paris showed up. I couldn't tell him what happened. He'd probably have flipped and committed murder."

Heather puts her hands on her hips and glowers. "Now Ryan has that TikTok video. Anything you do will seem like a revenge plot."

"That's probably why he did it—to discredit me. But there were a few people around when he pushed me, and one guy helped me get rid of him."

"Good. Will the guy confirm your story?"

"I think so. You might know him. He's a Pike pledge."

Her eyebrows shoot up. "What's his name?"

"Philip Meester."

She squints as if she's thinking hard about it. "God, I don't know if I remember him. But if he hopes to become a Pike, he *will* cooperate."

Heather has been dating Leo for a long time. I don't really get the sense that they're crazy in love like Paris and I are, but whatever they have going on seems to work for them.

"Okay, get ready. I'm taking you to the police station now."

"What?" My eyes bug out while my heart leaps into my throat and gets stuck.

"You said you were going to report Ryan. The longer we wait, the harder it will be to prove he did anything. Time is not your friend now that Paris knows he hurt you again."

She's right. Paris will do something stupid. I know it deep in my bones. Nausea hits me suddenly and so violently that I don't have time to run to the bathroom or the kitchen sink. I puke into the vase that holds the flowers Paris gave me. There isn't much to spew, since, thanks to the altercation with Lydia, I didn't eat lunch.

When I'm done emptying the contents of my stomach, Heather offers me a napkin.

I wipe my mouth, and then say, "I know what I have to do. I'm just afraid no one will believe me."

She narrows her eyes. "Do you seriously think you were Ryan's first victim? Trust me, the moment you report him, more girls will come out of hiding and do the same. I know at least two that I suspect were victimized by him."

I blink fast as I process her words. "How would you know that?"

"I'm head cheerleader, and I'm dating the president of a fraternity. I run in different circles than you, and drunk girls talk."

"Okay, but since when do you have information that Ryan is a bastard?"

Her shoulders sag as she sighs. "Don't hate me, but I heard those rumors while you were dating him."

"Why didn't you *tell* me?" I shriek.

"A few reasons. I didn't know if they were true, and Ryan seemed to treat you well. And you needed to get over Paris."

I cover my face with my hands. "I had to go and pick the worst sort of distraction from him."

"I don't blame you for going for Ryan. He's the exact opposite of Paris—clean-cut and attractive in a cold way. In hindsight, he has the looks of a serial killer. But enough stalling. Go take a shower and get ready so we can nail that son of a bitch."

"Okay."

I head to my room, and when I'm alone, I call Paris. Maybe

if he knows I'm going to report Ryan right now, it'll stop him from doing something stupid.

He doesn't answer my call, and the invisible knife stabbing my chest moves deeper. I sit on my bed, barely able to breathe as I type a message to him. My hands are shaking, and I have to retype words several times to get rid of the typos. By the time I set down my phone and stare at the bedroom's closed door, I'm spent. The desire to curl up in a fetal position again and not move for hours is overwhelming. But I have to find the strength to do the right thing. Ryan must be stopped.

I'M a bundle of nerves as I sit across from the police officer taking my statement. It's a woman, but still, I feel like she's judging me and not believing a word that comes out of my mouth.

"Tell me again why you didn't report the assault as soon as it happened?"

"How many times are you going to ask my sister that?" Heather butts in. "Honestly, it's no surprise victims of sexual assault don't report it."

"I didn't want the stigma," I answer the cop before she decides to arrest Heather. "I know it's not a good excuse, but that's what I was thinking at the time."

"And then you encountered your ex twice after he allegedly assaulted you."

She keeps using that word—*allegedly*—and it's setting my teeth on edge. It takes all my willpower not to lash out at her like Heather is doing.

"Yes. The first time I was with my teammate, Sadie Clarkson, and the second time was when he caused this." I point at the cut on my face.

"And you said Philip Meester witnessed the altercation?"

"That's correct."

"We're going to need his contact details to confirm the story."

"Isn't part of your job getting his information?" Heather asks, not hiding her annoyance.

The lady cop gives her a nasty look but mercifully doesn't offer a retort.

"There's something else you should know," I cut in. "Ryan recently posted a TikTok video making accusations about me."

That piques the cop's interest. She sits straighter and arches one of her brows. "What kind of accusations?"

"He said that I cheated on him with Paris Andino, the guy who stopped the assault, and that it's been going on for years. That's a lie. I didn't start dating Paris until after I broke up with Ryan."

"I see." She switches her gaze to her desktop and types away. "Does he have any proof that he's telling the truth?"

"How could he have proof?" My voice rises an octave. "He's lying."

"I have to ask the tough questions, Miss Castro. Since the Me Too movement started, there's been a rise in reports of sexual assault, but unfortunately, some of those claims have been false."

"Oh, so we now have to blame a good initiative for that?" Heather chimes in. "Watch Ryan come back to say he's the victim."

"He's already doing that by claiming I cheated on him," I grumble.

"I think I have everything I need on my end," the cop says. "I'm going to ask you to follow my colleague, who's going to take pictures of your injury."

"Okay, and then what?"

"Then we're going to interview your witnesses, although I

have to say, Paris Andino's testimony might not hold a lot of weight, since he's in a relationship with you."

"That's bullshit," Heather blurts out.

The cop gives her another stern look. I'm surprised she didn't have Heather arrested yet. She's really pushing this cop's buttons.

"I also agree that it isn't fair," I say. "I wasn't dating Paris when Ryan decided that raping me was the way to handle our breakup. If Paris hadn't been there, Ryan would have succeeded."

"I understand your frustration. However, there isn't any physical evidence of the first assault, so it will be your and Paris's word against Ryan's." She links her hands and leans forward. "As horrible as it sounds, that cut on your face is the only solid proof we have that your ex has been abusive—that is, provided that your witness confirms your story."

"So, I'm lying until a stranger says I'm not?"

"You could have tripped on your own and decided to use the accident to get back at your ex for the video," the cop says matter-of-factly, like just being here wasn't already difficult.

"Okay, but when you get the statement from the witness, are you going to arrest Ryan?"

"We'll bring him in for questioning, but I have to say, I don't think he'll even warm the bench in a cell."

"Has anyone ever told you how *great* you are at making victims feel safe and heard?" Heather pipes up.

"Lying is not in my job description. Ryan Watergate is from a prestigious family. Do you know how many guys like him stay in prison for any significant amount of time?"

"Maybe if the police did a better job collecting evidence, they would stay in prison," Heather retorts.

The cop stands and signals someone behind us. That's it. Heather has gone and done it. She's getting arrested for pissing off a cop.

To my surprise, though, the cop didn't call for backup. She's called over the person who's going to take my picture.

Before I follow the second cop, I turn to Heather. "Please try to keep your thoughts to yourself while I'm gone."

"Don't worry. I'm done wasting my time."

Not exactly the answer I wanted, but when it comes to Heather, it's the best I'll get.

I follow the second cop—a short and chubby guy in his forties—down a narrow corridor and into a small room where there's a backdrop and a professional camera already set up on a tripod.

"This won't take long, sweetheart," he says, sporting a kind smile.

I thought giving my statement to a female cop would make the process easier, but she turned out to be a mean witch. This guy is already much better. And he's right—taking the pictures goes fast.

When we're done, he asks, "Does it still hurt a lot?"

"Just a little."

"And your ankle? Did you also hurt that when you fell?"

I shake my head. "No, that one was on me. Although, it was probably the reason I couldn't avoid hitting my face on that bench when my ex pushed me."

"We're going to get him, sweetheart. Don't worry."

I tilt my head. "That isn't what your colleague said."

"Don't listen to Officer Sanchez. She's a bitter old hag."

His comment makes me laugh. "Thanks for saying that."

He shrugs. "Well, someone has to say it. But don't tell anyone I did. She'll have my balls if she finds out."

"Your secret is safe with me. What happens next?" I ask again, because I'd like to hear *his* answer.

"You'll be assigned a detective who's going to call you again to set up an interview. You'll have to answer the same questions you already did, on top of more detailed ones."

"Great. I can't wait."

"Don't worry. The detective assigned to you will have experience dealing with your type of case."

"That's good to know."

Fifteen minutes later, Heather and I walk out of the precinct. Despite the second cop's assurances, I feel flat and depressed.

In a rare display of affection, Heather tosses her arm around my shoulders. "We'll get him, sis. I promise you."

"I wish I was as optimistic as you are. You heard that first cop. She didn't believe a word I said. And if Ryan is arrested, I bet his lawyers will use the same arguments that she did."

"Then we'll find another way to get evidence against him."

"Unless we catch him on camera, I don't see how. I have zero faith anyone else will report him if I become a laughingstock at school."

"We'll think about it tomorrow. There's another matter we have to take care of."

"What?"

"We need to cut a bitch."

27

PARIS

IT TOOK every ounce of self-control to hide the rage brewing inside me from Vanessa. I didn't want her to be frightened or concerned. But that meant dropping her off at her place and leaving right away. It killed me that I had to go even though she begged me to stay. The latch keeping the beast contained had already begun to loosen.

My foot is heavy on the gas pedal and I'm gripping the steering wheel so tight, my knuckles are white. I'm driving way past the speed limit. Maybe my subconscious wants me to be stopped by a cop, because what I have in mind will for sure fuck up my life.

Ryan is a dead man walking.

The music from the radio gets cut off by an incoming call. It's Vanessa. I can't answer—not when I've allowed fury to consume me whole. A moment after the call stops, a ping on my phone alerts me to a text message. I don't peek. I'm almost to my destination: Greek Row.

I should slow down, but I continue at almost the same speed. When a delivery van backs out of one of the driveways, I almost collide with it. I stomp on the brakes, making the tires screech. The seat belt digs into my chest as momentum sends me forward. It hurts, but I ignore the pain.

A guy yells outside. From the corner of my eye, I see him running toward my truck. He's not Ryan, but I'm past the point of caring. If he wants to start a fight, I'm game. The van is still blocking me, so I get out of the truck with the intention of continuing on foot.

"What the hell is your problem?" the guy asks.

He's close now, and that's when I recognize him. It's Leo Stine, Heather's boyfriend.

"If you know what's good for you, you'll back the fuck off." I start to circle around the van.

"Where are you going, Andino?" The pest follows me.

"None of your business," I grit out. "Get lost."

"Does this have anything to do with Vanessa?"

I stop suddenly and turn around. "What do you know about Vanessa?"

I'm sure I look like the devil incarnate, but my aggressive stance doesn't seem to intimidate him. He lifts his chin and holds my stare. "I know more than you think."

I'm beyond thinking straight. In a split second, I'm holding him by his shirt and off the ground. "Then you'd better tell me, motherfucker, before I use you for practice."

He loses his arrogant air. His eyes go round, and his face turns pasty. "What the fuck are you doing, man? Put me down."

"Not until you tell me what you know."

"I just know that Ryan is a piece of shit, that's all."

I shake him roughly. "Try again."

More shouts in the vicinity warn me of incoming interference. Yet I don't break eye contact.

"Let me go, Andino." He grabs my wrists and tries to make me release him. Fat chance of that happening.

"Not until you tell me what you know about Ryan and Vanessa. And if you think your frat friends can help you, you're mistaken. I can turn your face into pulp before they reach us."

He glances to the right and then back at me. "Fine. I know what Ryan did to Vanessa in the parking lot of Tailgaters."

All my blood seems to freeze in my veins. "How do you know that?" I grit out.

"Put me down, and I'll tell you."

As much as I want to keep putting the fear of God in Leo, I have to remember he isn't Ryan. I set him down and release him. He steps back and runs his hands over his shirt, trying to smooth the wrinkles I put there. His friends finally join us and form a shield around him.

"Are you okay, Leo?" one of them asks.

"I'm fine."

I keep my eyes on him. I might no longer have him in my grasp, but I can still break his fucking nose despite his bodyguards.

"I'm waiting for an answer, Leo," I growl.

"Let's talk inside. This isn't a conversation for the middle of the street."

"Wait. Are you inviting him in?" a second idiot asks.

"Yes, Blake. Do you have a problem with that?" Leo snaps.

The guy shakes his head. "No, not at all."

This is not how I envisioned my day turning out. I was dead set on ending Ryan, but I can't not follow Leo inside the Pike house and learn what he knows. I can destroy Ryan later.

I've been here before, but not during the day. The house looks different when there aren't disco lights flashing and loud music pouring from the speakers. The walls in the living area are a dark-gray-brown color, and all the furniture follows the same neutral palette. The best colors to hide dirt. There's a faint smell of beer and cigarettes under the fake scent of pine in the air. No amount of air freshener can mask that combo.

Leo heads for a black leather couch and drops onto it like a sack of potatoes. He points at the couch next to his. "Take a seat, Andino."

"I'm fine standing."

The two friends who came to the rescue linger nearby. Leo looks at them, "You can go now."

"Are you sure?" one of them asks, giving me a cagey side-glance.

"Fucking leave or I'll rearrange your face," I snap.

They glance at their president again for reassurance, which they get through a nod, as if he's a damn mafia boss. Once they're gone, Leo types a message on his phone before switching his attention to me.

"Start talking, jackass," I say.

"On the night Vanessa was attacked, one of my pledges saw part of it and caught the incident on his phone."

Just when I thought I couldn't get more furious, Leo's confession proves me wrong.

"Are you telling me that instead of helping her, he decided to record the assault?" I grit out while my hands curl into fists.

"I didn't know what was happening at first," a guy replies from behind me.

I turn around and see Philip Meester, the freshman who told me what Ryan did to Vanessa yesterday.

"You!" I'm on him in the blink of an eye, pushing him against the wall and wrapping my fingers around his neck.

"Paris, wait! It's not what you *think*." Leo jumps up from the couch.

Philip's face is already getting redder, and he can't talk with the way I'm squeezing his throat.

"You watched Vanessa almost get raped by that piece of shit and you *recorded* it?" I shout in his face.

His brown eyes are round and fearful. He can't answer with words, and he tries to shake his head.

"Paris! For fuck's sake. You'll end up killing him." Leo grabs the back of my shirt and yanks.

In a knee-jerk reaction, I kick back, hitting his leg.

"Motherfucker!" he blurts out. "If you don't let him explain, I'm calling campus police on your ass. Then it's goodbye football season."

I glare at him for a second, and then I release his friend, but only because now I'm going to punch Leo instead.

He walks back with his hands raised in a sign of peace. "Don't do something you'll regret, Andino."

"I was going to help," Philip wheezes, halting me and saving Leo from a broken nose. "But you showed up before I could."

"And you expect me to believe that?"

"I swear to God. I was in the middle of shooting a video for my YouTube channel when I heard the commotion. If you look at the footage, you'll see that I wasn't near them. I ran toward them when I realized the situation was serious, but you got there first."

"I've seen the video, he's not lying," Leo chimes in.

I turn to him. "Why didn't you say anything to me or Vanessa?"

"Because she didn't want to report Ryan." Leo throws his hands in the air. "I heard her loud and clear in the video."

I rub my face as I try to calm the fuck down. "Who else has seen this video?"

"I only showed it to Leo," Philip replies.

"And you still have it?"

He nods. "Yeah. Did she change her mind?"

A nagging suspicion comes to the forefront of my mind. Squinting, I ask, "Were you following Vanessa when Ryan pushed her?"

"No. I was following *him*. I bumped into him by chance in

the humanities building and overheard him on the phone saying he'd be late to a meeting because his girlfriend was being difficult."

His girlfriend. I can't believe that asshole is still referring to Vanessa as such.

"Did you also film that?" I ask, not hiding my anger.

"No. I didn't think he was going to hurt her when there were so many people around. I was wrong."

"And earlier today? Did you 'just happen' to bump into Vanessa by chance?"

His face becomes bright red, and guilt flashes in his eyes. He drops his chin. "No. I was actually following her today."

My protective instinct flares up, and the desire to hurt him returns with a vengeance. I never pegged myself as a jealous caveman, but I never loved anyone so intensely and completely as I love Vanessa.

"You'd better have a good reason for that, besides being a fucking stalker."

"Philip is not a stalker," Leo butts in. "He's a nice guy who was worried."

"Vanessa doesn't need a bodyguard," I growl.

He quirks an eyebrow. "Why? Because she has you?"

The comment was meant to hurt, and it does the job. I dropped the ball when it came time to keep my girl safe.

"What's going to happen now? Is she ready to report Ryan?" Philip asks. "I can testify about yesterday's incident, and the police can have the footage from the assault."

I don't want to keep talking about Vanessa's personal life with these two, so I just reply, "We'll be in touch."

"Where are you going now?" Leo asks, his body tense again.

"Don't worry. I'm not going after Ryan. That was my intention earlier, but sending him to prison will be far more satisfying than breaking his bones."

28

VANESSA

THE POLICE STATION is at the corner of a busy intersection, and it takes forever for the pedestrian light to turn to WALK. As much as I'd like to share Heather's enthusiasm about going after Lydia, I can't find an ounce of motivation now. She hurt me deeply, lied to Paris, and drove us apart. But she isn't the only reason we stayed that way for so long. That girl is awful, but I can't lay all the blame on her. If Paris and I had talked instead of bickering, we would have found out about her deception before now.

"It's not worth getting revenge on her," I say.

"I disagree, but she kicked your ass, not mine." Heather shrugs. "I can still blacklist her from all social activities on campus, and you can't stop me from doing that."

"She didn't kick my ass," I retort. "I would have fought back if Paris hadn't interrupted us."

"Right, your knight in shining armor. Speaking of which, there he is."

"What?"

I stop in my tracks, which happens to be in the middle of the road, and follow her line of vision. Paris's truck is parked on the other side and he's standing next to it, leaning against the door with his arms crossed in front of his wide chest. The air is already getting cold, but he's not wearing a jacket, so his impressive muscles and beautiful tats are on full display. I'd run to him if I could.

"Go on." Heather nudges me. "I know you'd rather ride back home with him than me."

Before I take another step, I turn around and hug her. "Thank you for coming with me today."

"You don't need to thank me. I'm just glad that you did report him."

When we break apart, Heather's blue eyes are brighter. She turns away fast, maybe to hide the emotion in them. I continue toward Paris, who is now walking over. Before I can take more than two steps forward, he reaches me and hugs me tightly.

"How did it go?" he asks.

I melt against his chest and sigh. "It was rough. I'll tell you everything on the way home." Pulling back, I tilt my face up and look into his eyes. "I'm so happy to see you though. You're like a balm for my tired soul."

He cups my cheek gently. "I'm sorry I missed your call. I... I wasn't in the right frame of mind to talk to anyone. After I calmed down, I read your text. I wasn't sure if you wanted me here, but I had to make sure you were okay."

"How did you know where I was?"

"This is the closest police station to campus. It wasn't hard to guess."

"I'm glad you found me. And I'm sorry I didn't ask you to come with me." I drop my gaze to the hollow of his throat.

"The important thing is that you decided to report him to the police, and you weren't alone."

I look up again, smirking. "You should have seen Heather. She gave the cop so much shit, I'm shocked she's not behind bars."

He steps back, leaving enough room for me to maneuver my crutches. "Come on. You can tell me all about it in the truck."

"I can't wait to get rid of these," I grumble.

"When's your next appointment?"

"Tomorrow."

He opens the door for me, and then takes the crutches from my hands and tosses them in the back. I wait for him to help me into the truck simply because I want his hands on me.

He quirks an eyebrow. "I thought you didn't like it when I assisted you."

"That was then, this is now."

Twisting his lips into a crooked grin, he wraps his hands around my waist and lifts me effortlessly onto the seat. Before he can step back, I throw my arms around his neck and cross my legs at the ankles behind his legs, caging him in.

"What are you doing, kitten?" he asks through a laugh.

"You owe me a kiss."

"Is that so?"

"Yes. From you, a kiss is the only acceptable form of greeting."

"I'm fine with that." He slants his lips over mine and coaxes them open with his tongue.

I pull him closer, needing everything he can give me and more. I'm needy and hungry for my guy. Perhaps this isn't the best place to attack his mouth, but after the day I've had, getting lost in Paris is exactly what I need.

He pulls back, breaking the kiss but not moving away. He rests his forehead against mine and whispers, "I love you so damn much, kitten. You have no idea."

"Oh, I think I do. Probably as much as I love you."

He steps back, smiling from ear to ear. I toss my legs inside the vehicle and wait for Paris to shut the door. The butterflies in my stomach are wide awake now, all thanks to that smile. My depression can't fight the effect Paris has on me.

As soon as he drives off, he reaches for my hand and laces our fingers together. We don't speak for several minutes. I'm happy to bask in his presence and his touch.

"Am I taking you home?" He breaks the silence.

"Yeah. What time is practice for you today?"

"In a couple of hours."

I nibble on my lower lip. That's not a lot of time to really talk about everything that happened. "You don't have class before that?"

"I did, but I'm calling in sick." He smirks.

My brows furrow. "I hate that I've become a distraction."

"Kitten, don't say that. You're the best thing that's happened to me in a very long time."

My eyes prickle, and I keep them focused on the road. "I can say the same about you. I can't wait until this ordeal with Ryan is over."

He squeezes my hand. "About that... I have news."

My heart tightens. "You didn't hurt him, did you?"

"No. I wanted to, and I went looking for him on Greek Row, but I ended up having a chat with Leo Stine and Philip Meester instead."

"Oh? What about?"

"Philip caught your assault on camera."

I take a sharp breath as I process his words. "How?"

"He was shooting a video for his YouTube channel when you and Ryan came into the shot. He wasn't near, but it seems he managed to record it. I didn't watch the video, so I'm taking his word for it."

I blink fast, fighting the tears that are threatening to spill at any moment. "There's evidence that Ryan..." A lump prevents me from continuing. I look out the window, pressing a fist against my lips as I try to hold myself together.

"Hell, I should have waited until we were home to tell you. I thought you would be—"

"Happy?" I turn toward him.

The truck slows down until it comes to a complete stop. He puts it in park and looks at me. I don't even know if he found a place to park or if we're at a red light. My attention is solely on him.

"No, not exactly happy. Relieved? Now that bastard can't lie and say the assault never happened. You can send him to jail."

"Knowing that there's a video of the lowest moment of my life, and that it will be seen by many strangers until this is all over, makes me feel violated."

His anguished expression only worsens with my confession. "Kitten..."

"Maybe one day I'll be glad that Philip was there, but I'll feel relief only when Ryan is behind bars."

He reaches for my face and gently runs his fingers over my hairline. "I'll be there for you, kitten, every day, and in every way you need me."

29

VANESSA

A PHONE RINGS somewhere in the distance, waking me before I'm ready. I don't move from my current position, though. I'm too comfortable, resting my head against Paris's warm chest. His arm tightens around my shoulder.

"Who's calling at this ungodly hour?" he grumbles.

"It's not my phone."

"I know. That's my father's ringtone."

The shrill stops finally, but the damage is done. I'm awake, but so is Paris—all of him. I run my fingers down his abs until I reach the tip of his erection.

"Since we're up..." I say before I slide down his body.

"Hmm, that's a much better way to wake up."

Unfortunately, I don't make it to my destination before his phone rings again. It's a different ringtone this time, meaning someone else is calling him. That's never a good sign in my book, and considering everything that's happening in our lives, we can't ignore it.

I prop myself up. "Maybe you should answer it."

He spares a couple seconds staring at me before he sighs, "You're right." His brows furrow when he sees the number. "It's Danny." He puts the call on speaker. "Hey, man. Why are you calling so early?"

"I take it you haven't seen it yet."

"Seen what?" He sits up fast, his entire body tense, as if he's bracing for a storm.

"Lydia posted a video last night on TikTok. It's bad, bro. You need to watch it."

"It's rubbish," Sadie pipes up in the background. "Anyone with a brain could tell her tears were fake."

Shit. I *knew* that snake wouldn't leave things alone. I grab my phone and open the app. "What's her account handle?"

A second later, I receive a text from Sadie with the link.

Paris and I watch it on my phone together while he keeps Danny on the line. Honestly, I think he forgot he was on a call. The video is three minutes long, and she spends half the time talking about her mental health issues—a.k.a. building sympathy—and the other half talking trash about Paris and blaming him for her relapse. She ends the video saying she doesn't know if she'll be able to survive that betrayal.

"I can't believe she's done that after what you went through with Cory. She can't be that evil, right?"

"She's totally pulling a *13 Reasons Why* move," Sadie replies to my outburst.

Paris rests his head in his hands. "She might actually hurt herself."

I throw my arm around his shoulders and pull him closer to me. "Maybe. But you can't let her make you feel guilty about her decisions. The video she posted on TikTok was malicious, but it's also a cry for help—and she needs a professional, not you. She wants everyone to hate you, and that's not the move of a stable person."

"I have to call my dad back."

"Okay, man. Keep us posted," Danny says before he ends the call.

I drop my arm from Paris's shoulder and move to give him some space, but he reaches for my hand and stops me from going too far as he returns his father's call.

"Hey, Dad."

"I don't know what happened, son, but you need to help us find Lydia."

"What do you mean, find her?"

"She's missing. Her parents just left our house after yelling at us for half an hour. They're blaming you for her meltdown. Were you seriously cheating on her with that Castro girl?"

I bristle. Paris's hold on my hand tightens.

"I *never* cheated on Lydia," he grits out. "And stop calling Vanessa 'that Castro girl.' She's my girlfriend, Dad, and I love her."

My heart swells with emotion despite the shitty situation.

"Oh. Well, don't tell your mother yet. She isn't in any state to receive that news. Despite your current relationship situation, you must find Lydia. You need to salvage your reputation somehow."

He swallows hard. "So that's what this is all about. You're concerned about my reputation."

"I don't want anything to happen to the girl, but you're my son—my priority is to make sure *you* are okay. I don't believe for a second you're responsible for whatever's going on with her. But I've read some of the comments people left on her video. They hate you, son."

We purposely avoided the comments, but I imagine they're vile. I loathe people sometimes. Keyboard warriors and their digital pitchforks can rot in hell.

"How do they know she's gone? Couldn't she be avoiding their calls?"

"Maybe. But they're worried. You know more about her habits than they do. Do you know where she could be?"

I watch Paris closely, hating how this conversation is affecting him. His face is pinched, and the hard set of his jaw tells me he's wrestling with a guilt he shouldn't feel.

"I'm not sure. I have to get my head on straight. I'll call if I have news."

"Okay, son. I'll do the same if I hear anything."

Paris ends the call. His shoulders sag, and he stares at his phone without moving. There's a knot in my chest now. I don't know how to help him, and I'm afraid anything I say will sound insincere or self-serving. I hate Lydia for what she's doing to us, but I don't want her to die.

"Do you have any idea where she would go?" I ask softly.

He turns to me, revealing bright, anguished eyes. "No. Isn't that terrible? I dated her for years, and I don't fucking know where she would go."

The loud noise of a door banging shut prevents me from saying something that would only make things worse.

"Vanessa?" Heather calls out. "Are you decent?"

"Just a second." I jump out of bed and get dressed quickly.

When Paris doesn't make a move to at least put on his underwear, I toss his boxers at him. "Get dressed, unless you want to give Heather a peep show."

He blinks fast, and then replies, "Uh, no to that."

"I'm coming in," Heather announces a second before she opens the door.

"What's going on?" I ask, noticing she's still wearing the same outfit as yesterday. She has clothes at Leo's, so if she spent the night there, she'd have changed.

"What's going on is that I was right to follow my instincts. You can thank me later."

I lift my hands. "Thank you for what exactly?"

"I wasn't happy with your attitude about not giving that

snake some sort of punishment, so I decided to take matters into my own hands."

"Oh my god, Heather. What did you do?" I ask, worried that she's responsible for Lydia's disappearance.

Paris is standing now, a giant who's tenser than before.

Heather waves a hand dismissively. "Oh relax. I didn't kill the bitch. I had a feeling she was going to pull one final stunt to destroy you and Paris, so I stalked her place and all her social media accounts. Then she posted that TikTok video." She shakes her head. "Classic manipulator move."

"Cut to the chase, Heather," Paris butts in. "Do you know where she is?"

"Sure do." She lifts her phone and presses play on the video already loaded on her screen.

A grainy but recognizable video of Lydia riding a mechanical bull at some bar plays for us as a crowd of drunks cheers her on.

"I followed her to a dive bar off campus, can't remember the name now. She was partying without a care in the world. I have more videos like this, including one where she's making out with some random dude."

"That just proves she didn't harm herself, but people can argue she was acting out because she was depressed," I say.

Heather smiles like a fiend. "I got close enough to capture part of her conversation. I got a confession, sis. She fully admitted to the dude she was with that she ruined her ex's life."

"Can I see that video?" Paris asks, his voice cold and tight.

She plays it for him. It's only a snippet, but it does contain her confession.

Paris's cheeks hollow as he watches it, and by then, his jaw is locked tight. "Thanks." He returns Heather's phone. "What are you planning to do with it?"

"It's up to you. I have a TikTok video in my drafts, ready to go. Just say the word."

His eyes narrow a fraction before he replies, "Load it up."

30

VANESSA

THE FIRE LYDIA started by posting that bullshit TikTok was quickly put out once Heather posted her video of Lydia confessing to lying about the whole thing. That bitch's plan to make people hate Paris backfired, and she ended up earning all the hate herself.

However, the next few days aren't blissful. I'm a stressed-out mess, thanks to waiting for an update on my case against Ryan. The day after I reported that scumbag, Paris and I returned to the station so he could give his statement. I also wanted the cops to know about Philip's video.

Because Ryan hasn't been arrested yet, I maintain my decision to keep my assault a secret from the team. I don't want any distractions. This is an important game for us. We're playing our biggest rival, and I feel guilty enough that I'm warming the bench instead of leading them on the field.

Paris's game started earlier, but I didn't go. As much as I'd love to support him, my team needs me more than he does.

There are five minutes left on the clock in the second half, and we have yet to score. We're tied at 0–0. My replacement is a talented freshman, Ginny Sanders, without much experience. She hasn't yet jelled with the team—Sadie already yelled at her a few times for losing the ball to our adversaries while attempting to pass. Charlotte, our second midfielder, is doing everything she can to compensate.

Despite my promise to Paris to take it easy today, I'm on my feet, shouting encouragement to the team. The Ravens are on the attack, Ginny has the ball, and Sadie is positioned perfectly to receive the pass and score. But Ginny touches the ball wrong, sending it directly to the only defensive player between Sadie and the goal. The defensive player deflects the shot, earning us a corner kick at least.

Sadie's face is red, and not because she's been running. She's ready to go off on the poor girl again, but arguing among ourselves won't help us win the game.

"Sadie!" I shout, trying to draw her attention to me.

She turns in my direction. I signal quickly with my hands, urging her to calm down. In a typical Sadie move, she looks up at the sky and groans, before running toward the goal to get in position.

Joanne, our second striker, doesn't waste any time and sprints toward the corner to make the kick. My heart is pounding fast and hard against my rib cage, and I don't dare breathe. This is our chance to score. Sadie and Charlotte are in position, but Sadie, the tallest, has the better chance of touching the ball.

The whistle blows, and then Joanne fires the ball toward the goal box in a perfect arch. I hold my breath, gripping my crutches tight. Several players jump all at once, but it's Sadie's blonde head that connects with the ball and sends it straight toward the goal. The keeper tries to block, stretching her arms to the max to no avail.

The ball touches the net, and a yell rips out of my throat. It's swallowed by thousands more from the crowd. Sadie and Charlotte run to the sideline to celebrate with me, almost knocking me down with their enthusiasm. The game isn't over yet, and now the opposing team will be more aggressive than before.

I wish I could run along the sideline to keep up with the players. It takes a herculean effort to remain in one spot. My gaze is glued to the field, my attention solely on the game, and for that reason, I don't notice anyone approach me from behind. Strong arms snake around my waist and pull me against a solid body, making me yelp.

"How's it going, kitten?" Paris asks close to my ear.

"Oh my god. You scared me," I reply through a laugh.

He chuckles. "Didn't mean to."

"Did you guys just score?" Danny stops next to me.

"Yeah. Didn't you see?"

"We literally just stepped onto the field when the crowd went wild," Paris replies.

"It was awesome. Sadie scored."

"Ah man. And I missed that?" Danny looks crestfallen.

"I'm sure you can watch the replay," I say. "How was your game?"

Paris releases me but only to switch positions and stand next to me. He keeps one of his arms wrapped around my waist. "You didn't keep up with the score?"

My face becomes hotter as shame surges through me. "No. I'm sorry. I've been too absorbed in this game."

The corners of his lips twitch upward. "I know. I was just yanking your chain. We won by a landslide, 27 to 3."

"That's awesome." I rise on my tiptoes and pull his face to mine for a kiss.

Like always, it's electrifying and makes my entire body tingle with desire. For that reason alone, I ease back quickly.

Attacking his mouth while the Ravens are still playing isn't a good example for the team.

I return my full attention to the girls. As I predicted, the opposing team becomes more aggressive, but our defense holds. I relax only when the referee whistles to signify the end of the game.

Danny runs to Sadie and scoops her into his arms. A lazy smile blossoms on my face. They're so adorable together.

Paris kisses the side of my forehead. "In a few weeks, that'll be us celebrating."

I turn to him, beaming from ear to ear. "I can't wait."

It takes a few minutes for our celebration on the field to end. Per tradition, the MVP of the game—Sadie—gets soaked in what's left of the icy water. Because she's a fiend, she pulls me to her side while the dunking is happening, meaning I get drenched as well. I'm caught between cursing at her and laughing from the belly up.

During all this, there's a moment when my gaze connects with Paris, who's hanging with Danny far from the splash zone. His lips are turned slightly upward, as if he's trying not to laugh, but his amused eyes give him away.

I break away from the girls and walk over. "What are you smiling at?"

"You."

"Oh yeah?" I drop the crutches and jump into his arms, getting him wet too.

He picks me up and slants his mouth over mine. His kiss is demanding, hungry, and possessive, making me forget there are thousands of witnesses. A throat clearing nearby interrupts our moment. I pull back but hold Paris's heated gaze.

"I hope you're ready to do some explaining," Heather says.

Wait. My *sister* came to a Ravens game?

I slide off Paris and turn to her. "Wow, you're here, and I'm not even playing today."

She smirks. "When I heard Paris was coming, I knew I had to be here."

Leeriness takes hold. "Why?"

She hikes her thumb and points at a spot in the stands. Our parents are there, in their usual seats near the field, but unlike any other day, they aren't happy. I can see their frowns from where I stand.

"Hell, I didn't know they were still planning to come despite me being on the bench."

"Your surprise is amusing. Of course they came. They're the Ravens' biggest fans. Duh."

"I didn't know," Paris pipes up. "You could have given *me* the heads-up. I would have refrained from making out with Vanessa in front of them."

Heather laughs. "Why would I do that? The main reason I came was to watch my folks go apeshit on your asses."

"I hate you," I grumble. "Remember, sis. Payback is a bitch."

31

PARIS

I SHOULD HAVE KNOWN Heather was up to no good when she said she'd come to the Ravens game. She's always had a penchant for making things go up in flames while she watches the mayhem calmly with a wicked grin on her face.

If I'd known their parents would be in attendance, I'd have behaved better. Surprisingly, when I go to say hello to them, they don't bite my head off. Maybe they don't want to make a scene in front of an audience.

When Vanessa invites me to come to dinner with them, her parents' death glares intensify up to eleven. If looks could kill, I'd be dead. But I'm unable to deny any request she makes— she has me wrapped around her finger good, and I'm totally fine with it.

That's how I find myself at Trattoria La Nonna, sitting across from Mr. Castro, who can't stop glaring at me. I've never been more uncomfortable in my life. Vanessa is next to me, but not even her warm hand on my thigh is helping me relax. Maybe it's doing the opposite.

"So, you're really determined to piss off everyone to be together," he says.

"Dad, come on. Why should we cater to the whims of others? Paris makes me happy."

Her mother shakes her head. "Every time he comes into your life, you get hurt, *filha*. You can't blame us for being concerned."

"I never meant for Vanessa to get hurt, Mrs. Castro. I love her with all my heart," I reply.

Vanessa squeezes my leg in response, making me turn to look at her. I can't help the smile that tugs at the corners of my lips. I'm under fire here, and she still makes me grin like a fool.

"*Love* her..." Her father snorts. "You just started going out. How can you make such a claim?"

My smile vanishes, but I'm not angry. I'm dead serious when I lock gazes with him. "I've loved her since we were kids, Mr. Castro. Sure, life and other people got in the way, but my feelings for her never faded. They were just dormant."

"What about that awful girl you dated for years? Did you forget her just like that?" Vanessa's mother snaps her fingers.

"She's an easy one to forget," Heather pipes up. "Lydia doesn't have an interesting bone in her body. No wonder she had to resort to deceit and manipulation to hold on to Paris for so long."

I don't want to talk about Lydia. I don't know yet how I feel about her. It was upsetting to learn she lied to me, but I can't ignore the fact that she's not healthy and needs medical attention. I definitely don't hate her, but I do pity her, and I want her to be well.

"Lydia is not an issue, Mom. But there is something I'd like to tell you." Vanessa tenses.

There's only one topic that would make her react like that. I cover her hand with mine and squeeze, hoping it will give her some support. This won't be an easy conversation.

Her parents sit straighter in their chairs.

"What is it, honey?" her dad asks.

"I never told you why Ryan wasn't at Lorena's wedding. I broke up with him the night before, and..." She drops her chin, letting out a heavy exhale.

I don't know what else to do except keep holding her hand. It breaks my heart to watch the love of my life struggle to tell her parents about that nightmarish evening.

"And what?" her mom probes.

"He attacked me."

Mr. Castro's eyes go round, and his face contorts into an expression of pure rage in the blink of an eye. "What do you mean he *attacked* you?" he grits out.

"He tried to..." Vanessa wipes the corners of her eyes.

"Say no more," her mother cuts in.

"You're not going to even let her finish?" Heather retorts, her voice rising an octave.

Hell, is she going to cause a scene? I hope not.

"That's not what I'm doing," Mrs. Castro replies. "Look at your poor sister. I know what she wants to say, and I'm sparing her."

"He tried to rape me," Vanessa finally blurts out.

A long stretch of silence follows. Her parents don't blink, don't move.

"That son of a bitch," her father says in a voice that's dangerously low. "Did you report him, honey? I hope you did, because I have half a mind to make sure he won't be able to take a piss standing."

Whoa. I had no idea Mr. Castro had a dark side. I thought he was the level-headed one in her parents' relationship.

"I came close to it," I chime in.

Mr. Castro's expression of pure rage morphs into something

else, and maybe I'm reading too much into it, but it seems his opinion of me might be changing a bit.

"Paris stopped Ryan, and he'd have killed him if I'd let him," Vanessa adds.

"Really?" Mrs. Castro's eyebrows arch. "You'd ruin your future to avenge our daughter?"

"Yes, ma'am. I would. In a heartbeat."

"Oh my god. From what century are you guys?" Heather throws her hands in the air.

"Anyway... to answer your question, Dad, I did report Ryan. We're waiting to hear back from the detective investigating the case."

"He hasn't been arrested yet?" he asks.

"Because Vanessa didn't report him right away, there's more red tape now," Heather replies.

"They have enough evidence against him, though. His arrest is imminent," I say with more confidence than I feel. The police are taking their sweet time to go after that bastard.

Someone's phone rings, and everyone at the table checks their devices, including me. It's Vanessa's, but she doesn't answer right away.

She glances at me instead, her eyes a little rounder than before. "It's the detective."

"Oh my god. Answer them," Heather tells her.

Vanessa presses the green button but doesn't put the call on speaker. "Hello?"

I can't hear what the caller is saying, so I settle for watching Vanessa closely. The muscles around her mouth are tense, and she looks a little paler than before. Those fuckers had better not be calling to say Ryan is going to walk.

"Okay. Thanks for letting me know."

She sets the phone down in silence. Her gaze is focused on nothing. It's like she's in a daze.

"What happened?" her mother and Heather ask at the same

time.

"Ryan was arrested an hour ago."

Relief cuts through the chains that were squeezing my chest tight. I toss my arm over her shoulders and kiss the side of her head. "Thank fuck."

Instead of chastising me for cursing, Mr. Castro adds, "Amen to that. I hope that bastard rots in jail."

"Yeah, let's hope so," Vanessa replies.

"And if he doesn't..." Heather waves her steak knife. "It's bye-bye, birdie."

VANESSA

I LIFT my legs and cross them at the ankles behind Paris's back, allowing him to penetrate me deeper. He groans against my lips and increases the pace, flattening me against the mattress. My headboard creaks loudly, and I'm sure at any moment Heather is going to complain about the noise. It's the first time Paris and I have banged while she's been in the house.

After dinner with my folks, we came back to my place. Heather went straight to her room, claiming a headache. I didn't have the heart to encourage her to go see Leo. I don't think she's happy with him, after learning he knew about Philip's video and didn't tell her.

"Shh. Take it easy, babe," I whisper against his lips.

"I'm trying. But your pussy feels so damn good, kitten."

"Maybe we should put the mattress on the floor."

"Next time. I can't stop now."

I can feel him swell inside me. The pressure is building for me as well. I don't want to stop. Instead, I capture his face between my hands and kiss him hard. It's a smart move, because in the next second, I come, and I can't climax quietly when Paris is fucking me into oblivion. Although with the racket my bed is making, I doubt Heather can hear me screaming anyway.

"Oh my god, kitten," Paris mutters before his body convulses with the power of his release.

I clench my internal walls, milking him to the max. He loves when I do that, but it's amazing for me too. Case in point, I come a second time, and the sensation is more bone melting than the first. Paris doesn't stop moving until a couple of minutes later, and by then, I'm pudding.

He rolls off me but keeps half his body covering mine. We're slick with sweat, our breaths coming in bursts. I'm in recovery mode, but I snuggle closer, wanting to meld myself into him.

"Thanks for coming to dinner tonight. I don't think I'd have been able to tell my folks about Ryan if you hadn't been there," I say.

"Yes, you would." He draws lazy circles over my arm, giving me goose bumps.

"I just want this to be over, but I know it will be a long process."

"And I'll be with you, kitten, every step of the way."

Like a real cat, I rub my cheek against his chest. "Thank you. I guess I need a knight in shining armor after all."

He laughs, and the sound is a delicious rumble that I feel deep in my core.

"I don't think you do, babe. You're my Éowyn. I'm just thankful that you let me fight by your side."

My heart swells with emotion. I didn't believe I could love Paris more, and here he is, proving me wrong again. I raise my head and look into his eyes, a smile tugging at the corners of my lips. "Are you saying you're my Merry, then?"

He matches my grin and cups my pussy. "I think I'd rather be your Faramir."

32

PARIS – *One month later*

PUCK'S WEDDING day has finally arrived. The ceremony isn't taking place in a church, like I originally thought, but at a beautiful location in Oak Glen, which is a couple hours away from LA. Puck told us he couldn't get a date soon enough in their church, but a family friend who works at the Oak Glen venue told him there had been a cancellation. It's in the mountains, and the views couldn't be more spectacular. I'd say they lucked out. The sun is out, but the weather is mercifully cool.

I fidget with my suit while Vanessa stares at me, grinning. She looks stunning as always. Her dress is a deep-burgundy shade that looks amazing against her tanned skin, but the best feature is how it hugs her curves perfectly. It's taking a lot of effort on my part to keep my hands to myself.

My brows arch. "What's up, kitten? Like what you see?"

"Always. But why are you yanking at your clothes like a five-year-old boy?" She steps into my space and fixes my tie.

"This doesn't fit right. It's too tight." I move my arms, feeling the fabric's tension around my guns when I do so.

"Stop doing that, or you'll end up with another torn jacket."

I grimace, stopping at once. "Right. I think I need to buy the next size up."

She curls her luscious lips into a devilish grin, and her eyes dance with mirth. "You're getting bigger."

Like the devil she is, she moves even closer, pressing her body to mine. Immediately, my dick stirs in my pants.

I narrow my eyes. "What are you doing, kitten?"

"Nothing." She rises on her toes and brings her mouth close to my ear. "The ceremony won't start for another half hour though."

I loop my arms around her waist. "What do you have in mind?"

"Whatever you fools are planning, forget it." Danny butts in, making me groan.

"We aren't planning anything," I retort, annoyed that he's interrupting my fun.

"Sure, that's why you're holding Vanessa in front of you like a shield." Sadie smirks.

Vanessa begins to laugh, hiding her face against my chest. "She got us there, babe."

"Since when have you turned into a cockblocker, Danny Boy?" I grumble.

He shakes his head. "I'm not trying to be a party pooper, but whatever idea you guys had, Andy had it first."

"What's Andy up to now?" Troy asks as he joins us with his girlfriend, Charlie. "Where are he and Jane, by the way?" He glances around, looking for his best friend and his sister.

Danny and Sadie trade a guilty look, and I connect the dots. That horny idiot. Troy might have come to accept that his little sister is dating Andreas, but that doesn't mean he wants to have a front-row seat to their sex life.

"Are you guys looking for me?" The man in question walks toward us, and it doesn't take a genius to know what he has been up to. Messy hair, wrinkled clothes, loose tie. Jane is more put together, but her face is a little red.

"Are you fucking kidding me?" Troy puts his hands on his hips and glares at the duo.

"Stop staring at us like that," Jane retorts, finger-combing her long blonde hair.

"You're not going to fight, are you?" Danny takes a step forward, ready to jump between them.

Charlie links her arm with Troy's and pulls him back. "No one is fighting. Come on, Troy. Leave them alone."

"Aw, man. I was hoping for a kerfuffle," Sadie jokes.

"Kerfuffle?" Vanessa raises a brow. "Even I know that word doesn't belong to this century, even in the UK."

Sadie laughs. "It doesn't, but it's fun to say it out loud, innit?"

I look over her head and spot a very tall and colorful woman coming our way—the wedding planner, a.k.a. Puck's older sister, Raquel. Her '70s-print dress is bright, and it hurts my eyes if I stare at it too long.

"There you are," she says, a little out of breath. "The ceremony is about to start, and I need my groomsmen. Come on, come on." She urges us toward the cluster of chicks wearing light-blue dresses.

I kiss Vanessa on the cheek. "I'll be right back. Don't go running away with a bottle of wine and spraining your ankle again."

She wrinkles her nose. "Never again. I'll watch where I step this time."

I scoff. "Oh, so wine stealing isn't off the menu?"

"Mr. Paris Andino, get your butt out there before I forget you're a grown man and smack you upside the head." Raquel points in the direction I should have gone already.

"Yes, ma'am." I sprint toward my friends, but I don't miss the laughter coming from Vanessa and the other girls.

I already know they are going to tease me about being scolded by Raquel mercilessly today.

VANESSA

WHILE PARIS GOES to the nearest bar to get us fresh drinks, I walk to the edge of the reception area, where it's much quieter and I can admire the view without interruptions. The sun set a while ago, and since we're far from the city, the stars are shining in the clear midnight-blue sky. I take a deep breath and let a sense of peace wash over me.

Puck's wedding is much better than the last one I attended. For starters, I have no family around to create drama, and I'm not dealing with a recent trauma. To be fair, it hasn't been that long since Ryan assaulted me, but I'm in a much better place mentally, thanks to the support I've received from my family, friends, and most important, Paris. He's been my rock, and the best boyfriend I could have wished for.

Ryan is free right now, waiting for his trial. I was a mess when he was released from jail, but thanks to a huge campaign on social media spearheaded by Heather, we managed to get the asshole expelled from Rushmore. It's going to be a while before the case goes to court, but at least I don't run the risk of bumping into him at school.

"A penny for your thoughts." Paris returns to my side, holding two glasses of champagne.

I turn around and take one of the flutes from him. "I was just thinking about life in general and how lucky I am that you're in mine."

"No, *I'm* the lucky one because you gave me a second chance."

"We were always meant to be together. Fate was just waiting for the right place and time to intervene."

His brows furrow. "I'd have preferred to come back to you in a way where you didn't have to suffer."

"Hey, turn that frown upside down. Everything happens for a reason. If I had to go through Hell to get to you, then it was worth it."

He sets his glass on the fence separating us from the twelve-foot drop and pulls me against his body. "I promise you'll never have to go through it again, kitten."

We both know that's an impossible promise to keep. The road ahead of us isn't yet clear of obstacles or monsters. I don't call him on it, though.

I cup his cheek. "Even if another detour into Hell is in my future, it won't be as daunting, because I know you'll be with me. And even if, for whatever reason, you aren't... in the darkness, I shall remember how your gaze brightened everything."

Paris stares at me without saying a word. Yes, I quoted the poem I wrote for Cory, because it expresses exactly how I feel right now.

He captures my face between his hands and presses his forehead to mine.

"And I won't be afraid, for I know you're with me." He recites the second verse, choking me up. "I love you, kitten. Always have, and always will."

I kiss him then, while tears roll down my cheeks. Typical Paris, always making me bawl my eyes out.

He pulls back gently and wipes the moisture from my face. "Don't cry, kitten."

I look into those beautiful blue eyes and see the promise of a beautiful life together. "These are good tears, babe. Very good tears."

Life won't always be easy, but I know Paris will be there for me, come rain or shine. He was many of my firsts, and he's now my forever.

** THE END **

Thank you for reading *Heart Smasher*! If you love this series and would like another book set in this world, please consider leaving a review for *Heart Smasher*.

If you're looking for another second chance romance from me, *Wonderwall* is your book. And guess what? The main characters come from the same city as Paris and Vanessa!

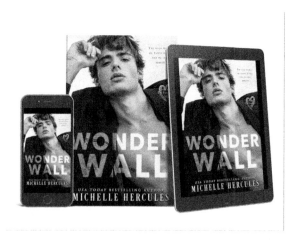

SEBASTIAN
If there's one thing I've learned in my life it's that fate is a

f*cking bitch. So don't get too comfortable, my friends. Don't think that just because you are happy now, your life is going to be an eternal parade of pink unicorns and sunshine. Once upon a time, I had everything a person could hope for—great parents, loyal friends, and Liv. She was everything to me, my best friend, the girl of my dreams, my kingdom come. And then bam! I had nothing. Sure, now it seems like I'm the king of the world. I have fame, an endless supply of beautiful women at my feet, and more money than I can spend in my lifetime. It's all meaningless without the girl I can't forget. So when I see her in the last place I expect, I don't think twice, I vow to get her back.

LIV

They say you never forget your first love, but I wish I could. Sebastian was the boy next door, the one who stole my heart, only to give it back bruised and broken. I've tried my best to move on, to erase him from my mind, but how can I do that when he is literally everywhere? There's no escape when your ex-boyfriend is on the cover of every magazine when his music won't stop playing on the radio. Was it a stupid decision to move across the ocean to the same city he calls home? Maybe. I was only following my dream. I didn't expect Sebastian to crash back into my life. He is different from the boy I once knew, darker, and much more dangerous to my heart. Resisting him would be the smart choice. I just don't know if I'm strong enough.

GET IT HERE

FREE NOVELLA
CATCH YOU

Do you want another swoony romance? Then **scan the QR code** to get your free copy of *Catch You.*

Pride and Prejudice meets Veronica Mars in this enemy-to-lovers romance.

Kimberly
I had always thought Owen Whitfield fit the mold of the

brainless jock perfectly. Group of idiot friends? Check. Vapid girlfriend? Check. Ego bigger than the moon? Check. As long as he stayed out of my way, coexisting with his kind was doable. Until one day our worlds collided, changing everything. He pissed me off so badly that I had no choice but to give him a taste of his own medicine. Little did I know that my act of revenge would come back to bite me in the ass. How was I supposed to know Owen would turn out to be the best partner in crime I could hope for?

Owen

I never paid much attention to Kimberly Dawson, but I knew who she was. Ice Queen was what we called her. She was gorgeous, no one could deny that. But she was also a condescending bitch, which was enough reason for me to stay the hell away from her. She thought I was a dumb jock, and that was okay until she came crashing into my life. Against my better judgment, I let her embroil me in her shenanigans, forcing us to spend too much time together. It was my doom. She got under my skin. She was all I could think about. I never thought I would be the knight in shining armor to anyone, not until she came along.

Scan the QR code to get your FREE copy!

ABOUT THE AUTHOR

USA Today Bestselling Author Michelle Hercules always knew creative arts were her calling but not in a million years did she think she would become an author. With a background in fashion design she thought she would follow that path. But one day, out of the blue, she had an idea for a book. One page turned into ten pages, ten pages turned into a hundred, and before she knew it, her first novel, The Prophecy of Arcadia, was born.

Michelle Hercules resides in Florida with her husband and daughter. She is currently working on the *Blueblood Vampires* series and the *Filthy Gods* series.

Sign-up for Michelle Hercules' Newsletter:

Join Michelle Hercules' Readers Group:
https://www.facebook.com/groups/mhsoars

Connect with Michelle Hercules:
www.michellehercules.com
books@mhsoars.com

facebook.com/michelleherculesauthor

instagram.com/michelleherculesauthor

amazon.com/Michelle-Hercules/e/B075652M8M

bookbub.com/authors/michelle-hercules

tiktok.com/@michelleherculesauthor?

patreon.com/michellehercules

Printed in Great Britain
by Amazon

30324102R00128